The Mechanicals

Wyvern Chronicles II

Other books by Nix Whittaker

Wyvern Chronicles
Blazing Blunderbuss
The Mechanicals
The Jade Dragon
Wyvern's trim and other stories
Ruby Beyond Compare

Wyvern Mysteries
Lady Golden Hand
The White Lady
The Lady Doctor

Kitsune Shapeshifter Series
Zero Foxes Given
For Fox Sake

Once Upon a Midnight

To family, far and wide.

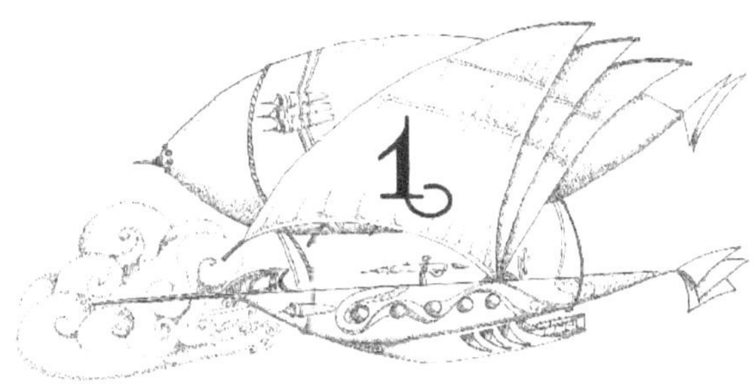

The shale skittered under her feet as Hermia crawled up the steep hill. Pain laced up her legs where the sharp rocks cut into her shins. She couldn't feel her hands anymore but she wasn't sure if that was the damage done by the shale or the cold. She could have taken the long winding path that led to the castle gates and reached the warmth and safety of the castle all that more sooner but Hermia was afraid her parents would have the road watched, they certainly had the village canvassed with their men.

It wasn't that Hermia's parents were monsters. They had been good parents. They had agreed to let her brother's tutors teach her as well when many noble families refused to educate their daughters. Her parents had thought education useless in a woman, but they had done it anyway because she had asked it of them.

Hermia had thought she could convince them that she didn't want to marry the arrogant Demetrius. No matter how important it was politically for her parents. She had been wrong.

Demetrius wasn't an odious groom compared to some men who had offered for Hermia, so they did not understand her objections to the union. It was difficult to explain that she wanted to choose her own path and not one determined by her parents or even society.

Over the years, she had made herself a small niche in her home, among books and silence. It had given her the illusion that she was free to choose.

Hermia hadn't realised how trapped she had been until the marriage had drawn close. When the wedding dress had been delivered, she knew her parents wouldn't change their minds. Hermia would have to take things into her own hands if she wanted a future that was purely her own.

Guests were already arriving for the wedding when Hermia slipped out disguised as a servant and made her way to the small village that serviced her parents' manor. She found someone willing to give her a ride out of the town. Someone who would not recognise the Lord's daughter under her disguise.

Hermia had walked the rest of the way to Duke Lysander's castle once the farmer dropped her off outside the small village that was at the base of the castle. When she had spotted her parent's men it had forced her to leave the road. She had been grateful for the boots she had purloined with the rest of her outfit. She would have been crippled if she had attempted this trek with the slippers her parents insisted were appropriate wear for women.

The Duke's castle loomed above her. Her breath puffed out in front of her in the setting sun. Instead of taking the path up to the castle she had been forced to take alternative paths. Unfortunately, none of it had been paved. She scrambled up shale, going backwards as much as she was going forward.

Hermia's hands were cut up from the sharp rocks as she clambered over. But she pushed aside any thoughts of the pain. She wasn't going back. When she finally made it to a flat area and glanced up and up some more. The walls of the castle were massive. It was built in the time of dragons when people had needed the stone to keep safe. Dragons were now their allies and the walls were only needed to keep out the Empire's enemies. It was certainly thick enough to handle any type of cannon the Roshians used.

A guard on the walls spotted Hermia and called out. Hermia put her hands up and waved them above her head a little too excitedly. She didn't want to be shot just because she had come up the side of the mountain instead of along the path.

When several soldiers ran out, she dropped her hands. They had a look of panic in their eyes and not one of murder. They waved her in but none dared to touch her. It was only when she was in the central courtyard of the castle that Duke Lysander offered his hands to her as he smiled.

"Ah, Hermia, my dear. Look at the state of you. When I suggested you come for a visit, I didn't expect it to be under these circumstances."

Hermia took his hands but Duke Lysander turned over her hands and blood coated her palms. It pooled from the small cuts from the shale. She had stopped feeling her hands a long time ago. They were blue with cold.

Duke Lysander frowned at her wounds and said kindly, "This will not do. Let my people look at you. We can speak in the morning. That is soon enough, in any case."

Hermia let out a breath of relief. "Thank you, My Lord." She hadn't realised she had been holding onto the worry that she would have nowhere to go when she rejected her parents' plans for her.

Duke Lysander's eyes warmed. "Please call me Lysander. We are friends, after all."

The look in his eye bothered Hermia but she couldn't put her finger on why the look disturbed her. The servants guided her through the castle to a lavish room. If she didn't know any better, she would have said they had known she was coming.

A servant cleaned her hands and bandaged them up. They brought Hermia food and she was left alone to rest. She slept for awhile but she woke late at night.

She stared at the ceiling for longer than she wished. Her thoughts tumbling all over themselves and keeping her awake. She knew from experience there would be no way to fall asleep now. Her hands throbbed with pain. Now that she had warmed up there was nothing protecting her from the pain. Her feet hurt as well but they had at least been protected from the shale.

Giving on trying to sleep with the pain she swung her legs off the bed.

Hermia lit a candle but it was difficult with her bandaged hands. She almost caught herself on fire, so she took off the bandages. Her hands were cut up but they weren't bleeding and as long as Hermia was careful, she shouldn't hurt herself too much. It wasn't like she was about to forget that she was injured with the way they throbbed even worse when she rested them by her side.

She tucked one up under her chin and without the bandages, it was much easier to hold the candle as she made her way through the castle.

Hermia had been here before and she searched for a particular room that she had only heard of but had never visited. The last few times Hermia had visited, it had been with her parents and they had certain expectations of her behaviour when visiting people. Along the lines of seen but not heard. Which meant she hadn't been allowed to peruse the library.

It didn't take Hermia long to find the large doors and push her way into the library. Shelves towered toward the ceiling in the massive room. All the shelves were filled with books with gold lettering on the spine. Ladders leaned against shelves so she could reach the top.

The only problem she had now was deciding which book to read first. The process took longer than she thought it would and she yawned by the time she tucked the book under her arm and headed back towards her room.

A clanking sound from outside made Hermia go to the nearest window to look outside. The moon wasn't very bright and it took a while to make out the shapes hidden in the shadows in the courtyard below.

They were enormous automata, like boulders who ponderously moved about the courtyard mindlessly. Hermia wondered what they were for as they were too large for most construction work or labour in the fields. Hermia shrugged it off. Many people had automata. They could build things and move things. She doubted they were to move things as they were just too slow but she could imagine they could build big sturdy walls.

She laid her hand on the wall of the castle. The coolness of the stone was pleasant on her painful cuts. She had only assumed the castle was old because of the size of the walls. But it could be a fairly new building if it had been made by those automata. Why would Duke Lysander want a castle that could withstand a dragon?

Her parents had never encouraged Hermia to bother with politics and geography as those were male subjects and in any case, Hermia preferred science and medicine. So she didn't know how old this castle was.

Maybe she could ask Lysander if she could look at the large automata in the morning. Their power source would be very interesting. He would also know how old the castle was.

Hermia was about to enter her room when a woman said, "You shouldn't wander around at night."

Hermia turned to see a stunning woman leaning against the wall further down the corridor. The woman had no candle or lantern so her face was obscured in the shadows but her voluptuous curves were obvious even in the darkness. Hermia held the book in front of herself as an unconscious defence.

Hermia asked, "Who are you?"

The woman moved away from the wall and stalked towards Hermia like a panther stalking its prey. "I am Helena. I live here at the castle and I can tell you it isn't always safe to wander around at night."

Hermia wasn't sure the woman warned her out of some need to be kind or for some ulterior motive. In fact, she wondered if the woman told her not to wander around for another reason that had nothing to do with Hermia's safety.

"I'll be careful," Hermia said cautiously.

Helena huffed. "Suit yourself but don't come crying to me or the Duke if you find yourself in a situation a noble woman like you shouldn't be in."

Helena turned and left Hermia standing by her room with her book still pressed to her chest.

Hermia wondered who the woman really was. She spoke with an accent but the words had been clipped and controlled like other nobles. Her dress was also of a noblewoman but the tone of Helena's voice said she didn't like nobles.

⊷━━━━━━━━━━━⊶

A boy delivered the telegram to the Blazing Blunderbuss while they were in a Middle Eastern port. It was such a rare occurrence to receive any correspondence so everyone looked over Hara's shoulder as she paid the boy and turned the message over in her hands. When Hara realised she had an audience, she decided she would take the message somewhere private.

That was more difficult than she expected. Even in Hara's room, Gideon followed her. She gave him a glare but he was oblivious to the daggers she shot his way and closed the door behind him. He considered her room his space as well ever since she had joined his collection. She had even tried leaving him in the capital but he had merely followed her. A good thing as he had saved her life but she had been hoping he would go back to his previous life as a professor of mathematics and leave her alone. She should have known better.

That time she had walked into her room to find him naked in her bed after he had flown to catch up with her. She believed he had been naked to punish her for leaving him behind. He was a dragon and his logic wasn't like her own.

Hara said, "Boundaries, Gideon. I thought we talked about this."

Gideon grinned. "You talked, I listened, but that doesn't mean we decided on boundaries."

That was an argument for another time. Her curiosity had her opening the message instead. She frowned at the few words and then glanced at Gideon. "It is from the

7

Emperor. He is summoning us as he has a task for us and in return, the Empire will pardon all my crew."

Hara's hand tightened on the message. She knew them becoming pirates last summer would have repercussions but they really hadn't had much choice. When they were threatened by the Roshian government to do their dirty work for them they had to turn to a life of crime or the Roshian's would send endless assassins after them wherever they went.

Gideon frowned at her revelation and she asked, "You know the court better than I. Do you think this is for real?"

"Yes, and that concerns me. They have not bothered with me in centuries," he said sagely.

Hara raised an eyebrow. "What about those guys at your house when I dropped you off? They were sent by the Emperor." When she had left him at his home, there had been two men from the court. One had been Harlen, Gideon's brother. He had been a surly type in all the interactions Hara had had with him so she could imagine Gideon didn't really want to see him.

With the way the other man had deferred to Harlen she had the impression that he worked high up in the Empire. Gideon didn't have much in the way of family. He had explained to her once that dragon eggs were abandoned after they were hatched. The only way they could keep their biological family was to add them to their collection.

He waved off her insight. "Oh, that was more about family than the court. It is unusual for a formal summons like this. And it is addressed to you. I think they might have heard that I've bonded with you and they are curious." Gideon seemed unfazed that his family all lived at court. Hara wasn't used to dealing with royalty.

Nobles, yes, as they had been her father's main target in his cons, but they had avoided anyone who had links to the Emperor's court.

Hara smoothed out the wrinkles in the letter from her tight hold and asked, "So you think it will be safe? This isn't a trap?"

"Not a trap, but it doesn't mean you have to drop everything to follow their summons. I never do. They often try to get me to come to family gatherings and I always decline. Even if the food is always good." He shrugged a single shoulder to indicate the choice was all hers.

Hara shook her head. "You made me captain of this floating zoo and that means I'm responsible for the crew. If this summons means my crew can some time go home, then I have to do everything in my power to see that through. I know you don't like the court but will you come with me?"

Gideon frowned and closed the space between them. He took up her hands and she let him. Not so long ago, she would have pulled free. Gideon was a very tactile person and she was used to his touches now. Technically, they were married but that was a complicated issue that Hara didn't like to dwell on.

He said softly, "It bothers me that you would ask me that question. Wherever you go, I will follow. You know that." He ran his thumb over the raised brand that ran down one of her arms. The sentence warmed her but she didn't want to admit it. She knew he was because she had been abandoned and used by her father so much that she didn't trust anyone to be loyal to her. That Gideon was loyal and willing to put up with her warmed her. But she still didn't trust it.

He had branded her and bonded with her in Rosha when a manipulative politician had shot her in the chest. Gideon had done it to save her life but he hadn't explained what it all meant. Hara had thought it had meant slavery but apparently it was more complicated than that. One thing she was sure of was that she didn't have to answer to him and he hadn't given her any orders. So whatever it was, it wasn't slavery.

Hara wasn't stupid. She had an inkling what it all meant but she wasn't ready for any of that. Men, in her experience, were only going to betray her and leave her behind. She felt just a shade guilty that she used this time to test Gideon to make sure he really was the man she thought he was.

Hara's opinion of men was low as her own father was a con man who had left her to be thrown into prison in order to escape himself. He hadn't improved over the years and earlier in the year had involved her in a plot to poison dragons and start a war between the Empire and Rosh.

The only man so far in her life who had been a positive influence had been her Opa but he lived in a small town where people made it difficult to be a woman and different.

Her Opa was a renowned engineer. In fact, he had worked for the Emperor's court while Gideon had been there. The two of them had even known each other before her Opa had met his wife and left the court for the small town on the edges of the Empire.

Oma had been an engineer as well but she had been afraid of crowds and open spaces. Opa had loved her enough to leave everything behind for her. Hara didn't think her Opa regretted it even for a moment. But he had enjoyed having the dragon in his home where they could talk about the old days and about Oma, who Gideon had known as well.

That didn't mean that the small town her Opa lived in didn't have its own issues. They had Alice on board who had been chased out of that town because of rumours started by an ex-boyfriend.

Gideon wasn't a man. He was a dragon, though that only made Hara more suspicious as dragons did not have the same moral compass as humans. What they thought was normal could be downright barbaric by humans. So far, Gideon had proved to be more human and noble than most of the men she had met in her life.

When the Roshian politician had shot Hara in revenge for upsetting the politician's plans to start a war with the Empire, Gideon had shared his life force with Hara to save her life. It meant that Hara and Gideon were now bonded to each other. Among dragons that meant she was his mate or part of his collection.

Hara didn't want to admit to Gideon that she actually trusted him and not just with her life but also her heart. At least he was being patient and would wait for her to confess her love. While he was just there waiting, Hara was determined not to take him for granted, either. Even when Gideon annoyed her. Usually on purpose for some bizarre pleasure, he got out of making her flustered.

⊷━━━━━━━━━━⊶

The crew waited in the mess for her to announce the contents of the telegram. They all turned their heads towards Hara as she entered with Gideon on her heels. The crew was so sure she would to share what was in the message that they didn't even ask except with their eyes.

Hara said, "We're going to the Emperor's court."

Alice smoothed her hands over her skirt and asked, "Are we allowed to?"

Murphy snorted. "If we aren't then we can always go in guns blazing." He demonstrated with a few hand actions and pew-pew sounds.

Talen frowned at Murphy's antics. "Or we can sneak in. It doesn't have to be an invasion."

Talen had worked as a thief for years. Even before Hara had known him. He had worked with her father when he had retired from burglary and instead collected information for her father, who had been a con man.

Hara waved her hand to get their attention and added, "We have been invited by the Emperor himself. There will be no need for guns blazing or sneaking. The Emperor wants us to do something for him, in exchange he will pardon us."

Alice looked the most excited by the possibility of a pardon. Alice, like Hara, had a family who she loved and would like to visit even if they lived in a town she found unbearable. Hara could understand Alice desire to go home. Hara also wanted to return home to her Opa. He was the only family she was willing to actually call family. Gideon had been the one to teach her that sometimes you can choose your own family.

Henry looked thoughtful. He had more to be pardoned as he had been part of the Blazing Blunderbuss crew before she had taken it over. When there had been real pirates. While he had been mostly used as slave labour the authorities had tarred him with the same brush as pirates. He wanted to be a cook but he couldn't do that when there were people out for his head.

She had thought he would settle down in one of the towns that had stopped in recently as he had been grumbling about being on solid ground. But each time he had made excuses to stay with them just a little longer. She wondered if he really wanted to return to home when he grumbled about solid ground.

Hara smoothed the letter out on the table. "I don't know what this favour is going to cost us so I need to know how far you all are willing to go."

Murphy patted his gun on his hip. "I'm in for some mayhem."

Talen glared at the gun happy muscle and then turned to her. "I don't care if I'm hunted because I'm a pirate or a thief but you still need someone to look after you." He eyed Gideon in specific but Gideon was always oblivious to those kinds of looks from Talen.

Hara said, "But if we head into mayhem, as Murphy suggested, will you still stick around? If I remember correctly, that kind of trouble was the kind you always ran away from."

Talen had, after all, left her just as her father had, though Talen hadn't known that her father would be rotten enough to leave her for the authorities to punish in order to save his own skin. Talen didn't deserve any special considerations, though he still insisted on trying to act as her father. He was here because he was a friend but she didn't need another father.

Alice said, "I'm in but I'm not a killer."

Gideon piped in. "Neither am I so we will avoid the blood shed while we head towards mayhem."

Liam said, "I like a bit of mayhem as long as it is worth it but I'm like Alice. Blood shed isn't my field of expertise."

Everyone looked at the cook, Henry, as the one who hadn't had any input so far. He coughed and rubbed his jaw as he thought. "I've been part of the crew before this who not only liked the Mayhem but the bloodshed as well. I'm not keen to go back to that but if it means being free to go anywhere, I want to, then I'm up for pretty much anything. These hands aren't clean so I'm not going to complain if they get a little bloody."

So he had been thinking about his past. Maybe this was the right thing to do. At least then Henry would have options.

Murphy patted him on the shoulder in a friendly way. "No problem, mate. Just point them out and I'll put holes in all the people you want dead."

Hara shook her head. "So trouble and mayhem is all right but bloodshed is to be avoided?"

They all agreed. Even Angel trilled her agreement from Hara's shoulder. She was a sentient mechanical construct which Hara had rescued from a border town but she felt she had as much say as the rest of the crew.

Liam said, "You know, working for the Empire really might be trouble. Working for governments has gotten us into trouble before. Look what happened when we became privateers for Rosh. We almost started a war."

There were ribald remarks to that but Hara tuned out and absently stroked Angel's head. The last time a government got involved they had been forced to become pirates. They had avoided having to kill innocents that time. Hara wasn't sure if they could always keep their hands clean of innocent blood if they kept looking for trouble. She hoped this summons was more auspicious.

<hr>

Alice and Liam saw Gideon and Hara off the airship when they arrived in Versailles. Hara said to Alice, "You might as well see what work you can get us. I don't think we'll be here very long but I can't guarantee how long things will take, so you need something that's flexible."

Alice nodded. "I won't let you down."

Hara saw the slight guilt shadowing Alice's eyes. Alice had once taken a cargo to be delivered to a very dangerous area of the world but Hara wasn't worried about that happening again. Alice had been naïve then and had since learnt more about the world and knew where they could take cargo and where to avoid.

"I know you won't." Hara patted Alice's hand. Hara turned to Liam. "Keep an eye on the others."

Liam grinned. He had grown up in the last six months and put on muscle and weight. He would outstrip Murphy soon if he kept putting on muscle.

Liam asked, "Who do you trust the least, Murphy or Talen?"

Murphy was a gun happy thug Hara had picked up in a shady port. The same port where they had picked up a Roshian Revolutionary who had betrayed them. Murphy was simple in his demands and what he wanted from life. He wasn't a worry.

Talen, on the other hand had once worked for her father, who was a con man. Talen was slippery but he had been sticking around as he had some misguided idea that he was in love with Hara and should make sure that Gideon didn't take advantage of her in any way. Talen was more confused than anything as he went from being jealous to being fatherly and dispensing advice that would never have passed her real father's lips.

Hara knew she would have to do something about the way Talen acted, sooner rather than later, but he was from a part of her life that was complicated and painful. Liam had been a witness to some of the more awkward encounters as Liam was her apprentice in engineering.

Liam wasn't really asking who Hara was talking about when she asked for them to be kept an eye on.

Hara shook her head and said to him, "Just keep an eye on all of them. I might get grumpy if they mess up my ship. You know I like a tidy ship."

Liam just grinned. He knew she was avoiding the issue.

On the ground, Gideon suggested they take a carriage, but Hara hadn't been to Versailles before and wanted to see some of it from the ground. Gideon had only shrugged and offered his arm.

Hara was waiting for a day that he turned into the men she was used to but he hadn't tripped up yet and she believed he might actually be genuine.

Gideon stroked her fingers with his own and asked, "Are you worried about court?"

She shook her head but she knew Gideon wasn't fooled when he added, "You know you don't have to worry. Dragons like interesting people and you are certainly interesting. The humans might be curious as to why you are there but they know better than to say anything."

Hara shook her head. "It doesn't matter if we are invited or not. These are many of the people who my father conned out of their wealth. I was part of that even if I was just a child and I'm worried some might recognise me."

Gideon snorted. "You were dressed as a boy."

Hara motioned to her clothes. "I'm dressed as an airship captain now. It isn't very different to what I wore when I was travelling with my father."

"Except now you are hot." He wiggled his eyebrows suggestively.

Hara laughed. "Only you would think that will calm my fears about going to court."

Gideon stopped her and turned her so he could look at her. He was taller than her by almost a head. He desperately needed a haircut. It flopped over his forehead and hid his eyes. But even she knew he looked at her with a golden, heated look behind his locks. Hara blushed.

Gideon said with conviction in his voice, "You are in my collection now and dragons look after those in our collections."

"Somehow being reminded of being owned is not very comforting." Her old concepts of ownership bothered her sometimes but she started to see that it was about connections rather than ownership.

"Not owned. Belonged. We are together. Bonded. The same. Not one above the other. Part of a collection."

Hara didn't want to admit it but it made her feel better. Even though her father was related to her by blood, they had never really been in the same collection. Gideon reminded her every day that they were family. Together.

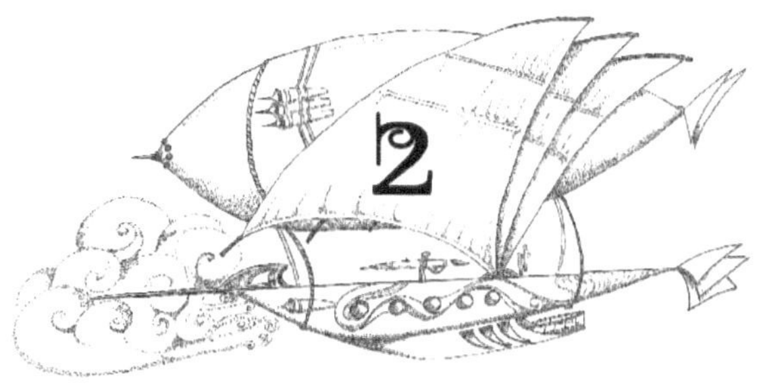

Gideon bowed his head to guard at the gate of the palace. The man looked him over with narrowed eyes but didn't confront them. Gideon had hidden amongst humans for a long time but everyone attached to the palace knew exactly what to look for to spot a dragon in disguise. He expected the guard to report his presence and Gideon knew a dragon would come to escort them soon enough.

While they were waiting, Gideon took Hara around the gardens. One empress had been fascinated with gardens and built one to rival anything in the world. It was an ultimate symbol of prosperity to have gardens which couldn't be protected from dragon fire and produced no food.

Gideon liked having Hara close to him and she still had her arm entwined in his. He wondered when she would realise she had fallen for him?

Harlen waited for them when they came out of the garden. Gideon growled when Hara let go of his arm to greet his brother. Harlen eyed her bonding brands and was stiff as she gave him a quick hug.

Gideon said, "Harlen isn't as touchy feely as I am." Harlen snorted at the understatement. Gideon continued, "In fact, I think he hates humans."

Harlen grunted. Hara glanced at Gideon. Probably to see if he was jealous. He was over that destructive emotion when he realised she was so prickly she would hardly let him in let alone anyone else. Especially when she had turned Talen down. She didn't know it but she was already Gideon's. He didn't need to be jealous and certainly not of another dragon. They would not interfere with a bonding, not unless they thought Gideon mistreated Hara, then they would take her away.

Gideon asked his brother, "Do you know why we were called?"

Harlen looked over Hara's shoulder at Gideon before he said, "We called her. We could have done without you."

Hara hit Harlen's shoulder. "That is your brother. You should behave like you are happy to see each other." Harlen glared at her but she ignored it and instead asked, "Or does it matter that you aren't in the same collection?"

Harlen's eyes grew sharp at the mention of collections. Gideon had only told her a little about Dragons and their obsession with collections and yet she understood more than any other human.

Gideon might be Harlen's brother but they had never been in the same collection. Harlen, though, was in the same collection as their mutual brother, who also was the father of the first Emperor. That made Harlen a prince and Gideon a strange political creature that no one wanted to touch. And Gideon liked it that way.

Gideon stepped up next to Hara, though he didn't offer his arm again and asked, "Are my rooms ready?"

Harlen's only answer was to turn and walk towards the palace.

Hara asked, "You have rooms?"

Gideon noticed some women eyeing him and they made him nervous. He shifted closer to Hara and she took up his hand without him even initiating the touch. The women eyed Hara's unconscious touch and turned their heads away to whisper to each other.

Gideon answered Hara's question, "Sort of. There are some rooms they set aside for anyone from the family. Usually they don't let me stay there but since they seem to be playing nice, I thought I would niggle them and insist."

Harlen could hear them. "You have stayed there before."

Gideon snorted. "We shared, that is hardly a luxury. You snore." He demonstrated for Hara, who chuckled at his antics. Harlen shot a look over his shoulder but Gideon ignored it. Harlen had always been good at throwing daggers with his looks.

Gideon, instead, stepped closer to Hara as they were guided through the palace. He didn't like the way the women looked at him.

He asked Harlen, "Who told them I was coming?"

Harlen glanced over his shoulder to look at Gideon for a moment and shrugged. "Not me. I couldn't care less if you are here or not." Harlen turned to look at the women and added, "But it is clear that your arrival was anticipated."

Hara asked, "Why would they care if Gideon was at court? I thought he had been here before and I got the feeling that he was only a minor dragon here."

Harlen snorted. "Not even that. Gideon is not in the Emperor's collection so he is merely a visiting dragon who has no rights or privileges. But Gideon is our brother."

Hara frowned as she asked, "Our?"

Gideon was surprised she had picked that up so quickly. Harlen frowned. Obviously, he hadn't meant to reveal so much of his connection to the Dragon Emperor. Gideon lowered his voice and said by her ear, "Our brother was William's father. His name is Erasmus but most just call him Emperor."

Hara turned a sharp look to Gideon, then asked just as quietly, "The Conqueror?" He nodded.

That had Hara looking between him and Harlen. She paled and he wondered if he should have told her. Harlen huffed but didn't add anything useful. Hara raised an arm to point to one brand that went all the way down her arm to her wrist. "And this means I'm married to you? That I am in your collection?"

Gideon nodded, feeling inordinately pleased that he had convinced her to be part of his collection. He wasn't going to let Harlen know they weren't completely at an accord on the whole marriage thing. He was relieved Hara didn't bring up that they had yet to consummate the marriage. She pointed to her herself and she went even more pale. Gideon reached out to steady her, worried that she might actually faint.

Hara shook herself off and some colour returned to her cheeks. She glared at Gideon but it was clear Hara would wait for them to be more private before she would vent. He liked that about her.

She liked to keep her feelings as close to her chest as possible. Gideon distracted her. "You should keep an eye on Angel as she is sought after here at the court."

Hara's hand automatically went to the clockwork dragon sitting on her shoulder. Hara glanced at Harlen to see if he would verify it. He didn't say anything so Hara was forced to ask, "Will she be safe?"

Gideon almost laughed. The clockwork dragon would be safe from other dragons as they only took things they perceived to be mistreated or misused. Angel was a very content little creature who had more sentience than seen in any other automaton Gideon had ever seen. He had been teaching the creature to count. It could never match him in its ability to calculate difficult equations but it was smarter than the average animal.

The crystals that processed its thoughts were clearly from dragon technology, though the clockwork was all human. If the rumours were right, then it had been a human who had made the small dragon.

Harlen said, "The women will try to steal Gideon and the men will try to steal your other dragon."

For the first time Hara looked at the women whispering in the corridors as they passed. She looked at Gideon and the look in her eye said one thing. Mine. It warmed him deep in his soul and he offered his arm and she took it.

Gideon said, "You make sure the women don't steal me and I'll make sure the men stay away from Angel."

Hara nodded her head sharply. "You have a deal, dragon."

⸺⸺⸺⸺⸺

When Gideon and Hara arrived at their room, it wasn't empty. There was a man lying in a chair. His legs over the arm and his head tilted back as he snored softly. Gideon didn't seem surprised to find the man as he turned to Hara and motioned with a finger to his lips that she was to stay quiet.

22

Gideon snuck up to the man. Grabbed his ankles and threw the man over the back of the chair. The man went down swearing and came up fighting. When he focused on Gideon, his expression changed and he hugged Gideon.

"Oh, man, it has been an age," the stranger cheered.

Gideon pulled back to have a better look at the man. "Only a hundred years. A small drop in the bucket for us," Gideon said nonchalantly.

The man patted Gideon's shoulder and turned to look at Hara. He stalked up to her like dragons usually did when they first saw her. He circled her and Hara placed her hands on her hips.

Hara asked, "Do dragons always do that?"

Gideon shrugged. "Don't know. I didn't."

Hara snorted. "That is because you were being kidnapped by Roshian Revolutionaries and were tied up."

Gideon's friend came to stand in front of her. "I am Janus."

Hara frowned. "I thought that was a girl's name."

"Not at all. Well, certainly it wasn't a girl's name when we arrived here," he said with some charm.

"That was centuries ago. You can change your name to suit the time like many of us do."

Janus rolled his eyes. "Says the man that chose his name almost a thousand years ago."

"Eight hundred and sixty-two, to be exact. I named myself after that soldier guy from the two river region in the middle east."

Janus gave a small, knowing smile. "Oh, yeah. I remember him now. He had that massive axe which he always carried on his shoulder and then accidentally cut off a braid one day when you surprised him with a live fish straight from the river."

Janus and Gideon laughed. Gideon said to Hara, "Janus and I were friends even back in our own planet."

The bright tone of Gideon's voice said that Janus held a much warmer spot in Gideon's heart than his brother Harlen.

Hara asked, "Are you two in the same collection?"

Janus snorted. "We don't do collections or collecting. That is barbaric."

Hara raised an eyebrow and Gideon coughed. "Janus, please meet my mate."

"Mate?" Janus' voice was high with shock.

Janus looked Hara over with a different eye. He saw the brand which peeked out of the sleeve on her arm and a little at her collar. Janus eyes were large as he turned back to Gideon.

"You really did it. You caved," His voice was incredulous.

Gideon shook his head. "I was only waiting for the perfect one. I just didn't want to be part of my crazy family's collection, though. So I avoided collections altogether."

Janus was quiet for a long moment. Angel chose that moment to move from Hara's shoulder and to search out their new room. She flew from Hara's shoulder and glided a half circle around the room before landing on the back of a chair.

Janus clapped his hands in excitement. "Who is this beautiful creature?"

Hara said with some pride, "This is Angel."

Angel tilted her head to take in the new dragon. "I knew a girl who used to make creatures such as these," Janus said with some awe in his voice.

Hara took an involuntary step forward in her excitement. "You know the tinker who made Angel?"

Janus took his eyes off Angel just for a moment to look at Hara as he answered, "It might have been her. She lived next to an aviary and so all her creations took on the habits of birds. She lived with half a dozen children as well. She was crazy as a coot to take on all those strays. She is doing better now but she isn't making these little gems any more so they are in great demand around the court."

Gideon asked, "You'll help keep the jackals off her?"

Janus reached out to stroke Angel's head. She tilted her head to better take the gentle caress. Janus said in a soft voice, "My pleasure."

<hr>

Hara stared at the tall ceiling of the ballroom. They had already been there two days and today they had been invited by Janus to go on a tour of the palace. Janus waved his hands expressively to take in the grand hall. The ceilings were decorated with gold babies with small bows and arrows.

Hara was glad they weren't invited to a real ball as she had no intention of wearing a dress and certainly not one that passed for fashion in the Emperor's court. Or at least she wouldn't without copious amounts of complaining. Those women could barely breathe let alone do anything practical with their lives while they were dressed like that. She wore stays and corsets but it was the tight lacing she abhorred.

Hara knew she might have to wear a dress to see the Emperor but she would put that off as long as possible.

Janus hummed and spun around slowly as if he were dancing with an invisible partner. Gideon caught Hara's hand and spun her around into a dance. He was surprisingly agile and coordinated.

Hara said, "I wouldn't have pegged you for a dancer."

He grinned back. "I did peg you for someone who leads."

She snorted and realised that she had tried to lead. She settled into his arms and let him swing her around the room to silent music and the off tune humming of Janus.

Hara said, "I learnt how to dance while I was dressed as a boy."

Janus said, "You would have been a very pretty boy."

Gideon snorted at the comment. Hara was surprised at the lack of jealousy from Gideon. He usually didn't allow males to make comments about her like that without pulling them up. He had certainly stood up for her against her father when he had treated her as merely a possession to be used.

While Hara had travelled with her father, she had dressed up as a boy. At first, she thought it had been exciting. As boys could do so much more than what girls were allowed. By the time she had hit her teens, she had realised that she was dressed as a boy because her father had needed her to complete his cons. He didn't care what she wanted or needed, only what he wanted. Unfortunately, that meant she hadn't learnt to do things women normally learnt to do.

Gideon frowned. "Do you want to talk about it?"

She glanced at Gideon, surprised that he had picked up the slight tone in her voice that said the memory wasn't a pleasant one.

Hara sighed and answered, "Not really. I just can't help myself getting mad whenever I remember all the things I used to do to please my father."

"He didn't deserve it," Gideon said intensely. He had strong opinions on her father.

"I know, but that is why I'm so mad about it. I was so stupid to think that I could somehow mean something to him."

Gideon's voice was fierce as he spoke. "You weren't stupid. A collection is supposed to care for each other. He did not appreciate you and that is why you are now mine."

Janus said, "You could always stay out of collections. I find that is easier."

Hara sighed. "It doesn't work like that for humans, Janus. We are born into collections."

Janus stopped dancing for a moment to place a hand over his heart in mock shock. "What a messy, horrible thing. I hope you escaped from your collection as soon as you were able."

Hara shook her head, not because she hadn't but rather because she didn't want to talk about it, and she would have said something along the lines of minding his own business in any case when one of the brave women who had seen them dancing approached.

She bowed like a man and said gallantly, "May I cut in?"

Hara stepped between the woman and Gideon. "Not now and not ever. Why do you women plague him? He has given no indication he wants to be with anyone else so why bother him so?"

The woman flushed with embarrassment and Hara felt bad. The woman had been rather brave to approach them but it bothered Hara as so many of the women over the last two days had been flirting with Gideon at every opportunity they could get.

Janus said, "Gideon was quite the catch in his day. He often had women flocking after him. He is, after all, related to the Emperor and a dragon. But I prefer the word plagued."

Hara sighed and said to the young noblewoman, "Sorry, I snapped."

The woman shook her head. "There are so few dragons that attend court anymore. My mother said in her day there were dozens. They treat their wives so much better than the pompous noblemen who come to Court to hunt wives."

Hara glanced at Gideon, who nodded as confirmation. Hara turned back to the woman. "Well, this dragon is taken." Hara grinned a little cruelly. "He is free though." Motioning to Janus.

Janus got a panicked look in his eye and started waving his hands in denial. "No, no. Don't even think about it. I might be unattached but I like it that way."

The woman flushed red again and Hara asked, as the woman seemed capable of whole sentences when speaking with Hara. "Why do you all want a dragon any way? They are really annoying? I mean bang your head against a wall annoying. They invade your space and never leave you alone."

Gideon chuckled at this and it was clear he wasn't offended. The woman looked between the three of them. "Well, with a dragon, they never stray and they give you immortality."

Gideon interrupted her. "Not quite immortality. We can still be killed and though we live longer here on this planet than on our own. There will come a time when our bodies' fail, though considering the tinkering we had to do to be able to travel here, it might still be awhile. My calculations are inaccurate though as I haven't been able to collect all the data that I would need to make an accurate prediction "

"It is all your fault, Gideon. You were the one who wrote the equations," Janus added helpfully.

Gideon glared at his friend. "It was that or become a fried and crispy critter on our own planet or worse, trapped underground."

Janus shuddered at the thought and agreed wholeheartedly, "Definitely not that."

Hara rolled her eyes. "See what I mean? Annoying. He spouts stuff like that all the time."

Gideon added, "Other dragons don't. Harlen wouldn't know a thing about quantum physics or genetic manipulation at the atomic level."

Hara knew a little of what he spoke about. Enough to know that they were not fields of study she was interested in. She liked to see the point of her work in more concrete ways Give her an engine or complicated mechanisms and she was in paradise.

Gideon was more of a theorist. But then he had been working as a mathematician at over a dozen universities over the years while he hid from his family.

Janus said, "Neither do I. Even though I do understand some of it."

Hara said with a triumph, "Ha, and he is just as annoying as Gideon."

Janus gave her some puppy dog eyes and said in a wounded voice, "You kill me, my love. I am bleeding here."

Hara was going to say something else to the woman when a courtier entered the ballroom. He saw them and rushed over to them. He handed Hara the gold embossed card and then bowed and left.

The woman said, "It is an invitation to the ball tomorrow."

Hara groaned. "Now I have to wear a dress."

Janus clapped his hands. "Excellent. Something that shows off your assets." Cupping his hands at his chest to indicate which assets he spoke of.

"Only if you want me to cut off your assets, Janus," Hara threatened.

Janus looked to Gideon and asked, "Aren't you going to defend your friend?"

"Are you kidding? She might cut off my assets," Gideon sallied back.

Hara was about to tell them off for being silly when Angel screeched and Hara turned to see her clawing at the door frame as a man tried to pull her out of the room.

Gideon said, "Let me."

He made his way across the room but before he could get to Angel, she turned her long sinuous neck towards the man trying to steal her and spat needles. He screamed and brought his hands up to cover his face.

Angel scrambled up the wall and sat on one of the ornate frames around a painting and chittered angrily at the man. He swore at Angel and was about to make another attempt at catching her when he saw Gideon heading towards him. He cut his losses and ran.

Gideon went to painting and said softly, "You can come down now, Angel."

Angel chittered a little bit before she hopped off the frame and glided to land on his shoulder. She couldn't fly very far as she was mostly a glider.

Janus said, "A marvellous creature, your dragon."

Hara smiled. "The clockwork one or the real one?"
Janus just gave her a knowing smile.

Gideon headed back to Hara. "The needles are a new thing."

Hara winced at his facetious tone. "We have been upgrading her. I didn't think she would need to use the needles here at court so I didn't mention it before."

Gideon shrugged. "You mock me for teaching her to count and you experiment on her. What did she think of that?"

Angel answered that by biting his ear. Before Gideon could even curse at her, she jumped off his shoulder and glided over to Hara's shoulder. Angel twittered in pleasure as she curled around Hara's neck and rubbed her cheek against her chin.

Hara patted Angel and crooned softly, "Don't worry, my dear. Papa Gideon won't hurt you."

Gideon rubbed his ear where Angel had bitten him. "But you aren't getting that treat I promised you, cheeky minx."

"Talking to me or the clockwork creature," Hara asked.

Gideon chuckled. "Both."

Janus hummed to himself as he took Hara on a whirl around the ballroom. It looked very different, with gas lights and candles to light the tall ceilings of the large room.

He said with a bit of wistfulness in his voice, "I do like to dance."

Hara had to smile at the tone of his voice. "I could take it or leave it, to be honest. I certainly hated dancing dressed as a boy and the dress doesn't make it any easier now."

Janus smiled. "You should ask Gideon to take you dancing some day when you don't have to be in a ball gown."

She studied the gold and yellow gown. It was beautiful but very restrictive and she had even left off a few of the petticoats. "I do appreciate the dress, though. I would hate to stand out at an event like this."

Around them the ballroom was filled the nobility of the Empire. Hara recognised some of them from her time as a lackey for her conman of a father.

Janus smiled. "Gideon once lost a bet and he had to attend a ball as a woman once. He made a terrible woman as he kept forgetting he was in a gown. He tripped more than walked. He certainly didn't have the grace you have."

Hara smiled as she tried to imagine Gideon as a woman and ignored Janus' flirting. Gideon would probably bat his eyelashes at people and flick his hands around gracefully as he flirted as a girl.

The music stopped and Janus said, "I think Gideon has the next dance." He looked at her face and he must have seen something as he said, "I never thought Gideon would ever take someone into his collection. He was adamant that it was barbaric and unnecessary but I can see why he changed his mind. You are an exceptional person."

Hara blushed at the compliment and muttered a soft thank you, though she wasn't comfortable with his words. They arrived at where Gideon waited on the edges of the ballroom. Others had asked him to dance but he had declined, so now he stood alone with a dark look on his face.

Janus said, "Don't look so glum, old chum. I have brought you your bride. Where is your marvellous clockwork creature? Maybe she can keep me company while the two of you dance?"

Hara answered, "We had to leave her in our rooms. We weren't sure if she would be safe amongst all these nobles. We knew she would cause a scene and we want to avoid that. The Emperor insisted that we be discreet. Having a dragon flying around shooting needles at dancers isn't very discreet."

Janus said, "I might go see if she wants some company."

He flicked a hand in a dismissal and wandered off humming to himself. Gideon asked, "Did you enjoy yourself?"

"Yes. Though you have to tell me, did you find it as difficult to dance in all these skirts as I do?" Hara flicked at the offending fabric.

Gideon let a smile crawl across his lips as it shone through his eyes. "I see Janus has been telling stories."

"What I can't understand is how you lost the bet in the first place." She let his smile become infectious.

Gideon sighed. "Janus cheated is how. We had made a bet that I couldn't make a contraption that could bridge over a river and then pack up and move on. He sabotaged it and instead it fell into the river. It took us several days to get it out of the water. The Emperor was not amused as it meant that his pleasure raft was stuck further upriver and he had planned on a cruise of some sort."

"This Emperor?" Hara asked incredulously.

"No, I've never met this Emperor. Most Emperors will only rule for fifty years and then step down. We still don't know how long the hybrids will live but it is well past normal human life expectancy," Gideon said offhandedly.

"So the ladies are right. You can give them a longer life. Even to their children."

Hara realised with stunning clarity why the women were so keen on Gideon and other dragons. The mortality rate for children was still high, along with other illnesses and accidents. Many children died young. A dragon's get would be healthier and stronger in a world where humans had been knocked off the top of the food chain.

The music started up again and Gideon motioned for them to go onto the dance floor.

Gideon's hands were placed demurely on her waist as he guided her around the dance floor. Hara had refused to wear the corset tightly laced so it wasn't completely uncomfortable. The gown was a deep gold so also not a terrible colour but Hara could have done without having her torso being pinned up so tight she felt like her brain might squeeze out.

Her consolation prize was that Gideon had dressed up for the occasion as well. He was in a deep blue and gold coat with a crisp white shirt.

Hara ran her hand over the brocade. "It was nice of Janus to organise these clothes."

Gideon snorted. "He charged me an arm and a leg. The shrewd bastard. He knew I would pay anything to see you in a dress."

Hara looked down at herself. "It isn't the dress per se, just that they are ridiculous to do anything practical in them."

Gideon said, "You look good in leather pants as well. Especially when you–" She hit his arm so he would stop where his speculation was going. He just grinned at her and she had to return the smile.

Hara said, "Do you think Angel is alright in the room?"

"Yes. We left her with toys. She'll be fine and she can certainly look after herself. And if not, Janus will keep her entertained for at least an hour." Gideon assured her.

They had spent a good hour explaining to Angel why she couldn't come to the ball. Hara wished she could teach the clockwork dragon to speak but there was nothing they could create that could make noises like a voice so Angel only had clicks and trills.

The music stopped and as they walked off the dance floor, a young courtier approached them. He bowed deeply. "Your presence is required."

This was it.

The summons from the Emperor.

Gideon had explained that the Emperor would most likely do business during the ball as it was an indicator that any business done during a ball couldn't be that important. Considering they were ex-pirates, the Emperor couldn't have them presented at court.

Hara caught Gideon's hand as they followed the courtier out of the ballroom and into the garden.

The crowd noise faded into the background as the courtier led them through the gardens. There was a wall of soldiers around the gazebo where the Emperor must be setting up his court.

Hara hesitated. She wasn't the kind of person that spoke to Emperors. What had she been thinking coming to court? Except that she had been invited and it was the only way to make sure her crew was safe and that they could travel into the Empire whenever they wanted to without the stigma of piracy over their head.

When she hesitated just a mite too long, Gideon turned to her. The concern in his eyes was enough to get her moving the rest of the way to the wall of soldiers. The two large men at the stairs of the gazebo glared at them. Gideon smiled up at them and Hara cleared her throat.

It seemed that Gideon wanted her to take the lead as usual. "The Emperor summoned us." She informed the two guards.

A voice from inside the gazebo said something and the two guards glared at them one more time before they stepped aside. Hara hesitated again. The courtier who had led them here had disappeared somewhere so there weren't going to be any formal introductions. Forward was the only feasible path.

Hara stepped up and into the shadows of the gazebo. The Emperor lay on a couch. He motioned for them to take seats. Hara sat down awkwardly on one soft cushion, wondering if she was supposed to lounge back as the Emperor did. Gideon sat next to her and lounged behind her. She glanced at him. Gideon slid an arm around her waist and encouraged her to lie back. It was awkward as she kept wanting to jump to her feet and bow but it was clear this was all supposed to be informal.

The Emperor surprised her by saying, "This meeting isn't happening." For a moment she thought he had read her thoughts but he continued on. "It would be a political nightmare if it was known I had put in my own copper's worth into this situation."

Gideon stroked her hair and she relaxed a little. At least she wasn't alone. Gideon said, "We are a little confused why you called us. The last I heard, I was persona non grata."

The Emperor waved his hand to dismiss the comment. "That was never my choice. That was grandfather. You know he can hold a grudge and when you refused to be part of his collection, he didn't want you to be near the rest of us. I've kept tabs on you. You do good work and that last grant was through one of my shell companies so thank you very much for figuring out how to build that silly bridge the merchants insisted needed to be built. But it means the two of you hold a very nice and disallowable position if things don't go as planned."

Hara found her voice and asked, "And what exactly is the plan?"

"My wife likes to play matchmaker. I don't condone it. Too messy dealing with love lives and marriages. But my wife thought this match was ideal and pressured the parents into making it happen. I let it happen as the girl has land which is on our border in the mountains and the boy's land is all close to the coast so it wouldn't give them any significant power to combine their assets. That would have all been fine but the girl is also my wife's niece. Family always complicates things."

The Emperor motioned for a servant to pour him a drink and he was silent as he took a sip. He waved his hand to indicate them and continued talking, while the servant poured them wine as well. "The girl, though, wasn't interested in marrying the poor boy so she ran away. That I couldn't care less about but the problem is who she has run off to. Duke Lysander married a lovely lady who had owned land also on the border of the Empire in the mountains adjacent to the land of my wife's family. The lovely lady died, suspiciously, but there isn't much I can do about it. The silly girl has run off to him. She probably has no idea that she is about to become a sacrificial lamb and she is my wife's niece, added to boot. So we need you to get the girl away from Duke Lysander."

Hara didn't blame the girl for running off. She wouldn't want to be forced to marry some boy just because his land was far enough into the Empire. If the young woman had been brave enough to set out on her own against family pressure, then Hara wouldn't make the girl go back. Hara said, "I'm not going to force her to marry the man she ran away from."

The Emperor waved his hand lazily. "I told you I don't care if she marries the boy or not. Just as long as she doesn't marry Duke Lysander."

Hara wanted to make sure they were all on the same page so asked, "And if we do this, you will pardon my entire crew?"

The Emperor nodded. "And I will acknowledge your collection."

Hara frowned at this strange phrase and turned to Gideon to see if he would clarify. He had placed his hand on the small of her back. She hadn't noticed until he moved his thumb. Making small half circles along her spine.

Gideon explained, "Many dragons came from our world to this one and to different places. When we settled, we decided we would leave each other's collections alone. We had lost enough in our own world and from the humans that we decided that fighting each other really wasn't worth the prize. But by then I had already disappeared to live amongst the humans so I wasn't there to sign the agreement. It has meant I've been in limbo for a while. I didn't really care. Most dragons abided by the agreement, even though technically I was not part of it. Part of the problem is that my brother has one of the largest collections and therefore a lot of power and he refuses to acknowledge me as family or as anything, really. He wants me to be part of his collection and not an individual. It's a power thing. He craves it. I don't crave power, so we clash. By the Emperor, who holds the second most power in the Empire, acknowledging me, I can now be officially part of the agreement."

The Emperor winced at the mention of the ranking among dragons. "I was supposed to be the most powerful and even grandfather agreed, but habits die hard and he can't seem to help himself. He has to be the boss. I can still wield a lot of power amongst humans and since you have bonded to your pirate here, it allows me to grant you this without having to step on too many toes."

Gideon shrugged. Hara knew he probably had a different perception of his brother but diplomatically kept quiet.

Hara asked, "So other dragons won't attack you?"

The Emperor said, "It is more complicated than that. There have been other agreements and treaties made between humans and dragons that all hinge on the first agreement made. Gideon could have attacked humans and eaten you and he would have been allowed as he wasn't allowed to be part of that treaty as he wasn't part of the coalition of dragons who signed the treaty. Dragons were worried that Gideon might get hungry one day and eat someone and create a political nightmare that would have sent dragons back into war with the humans. But once he bonded with you, he signalled he was like his brother. That he was willing to treat with the humans and can be part of the treaty. It is complicated but with you and my say he can finally be back with his family."

Gideon snorted. "That isn't a compliment. Who would want to be related to your grandfather? I have worked hard to stay out of his collection. Who would want to end up like Harlen?"

Hara had been side swiped a few times by Gideon's connection but she hadn't thought it all through. If the Emperor's grandfather was Gideon's brother and she was married to Gideon, then she was the Emperor's great aunt.

The air left her lungs suddenly and she coughed to hide it. Gideon frowned at her and rubbed her back. She shook her head at the concerned look in his eyes. She would have to talk to him later. She needed to know all the connections, otherwise she would be hit like this every time something was revealed. She was almost tempted to trade on that familial connection but it would be better to be on the good side of the Emperor.

Hara said, "We will rescue the girl from the Duke but I want a favour as well."

The Emperor raised a single eyebrow. "Even on top of all else I'm willing to offer?"

She nodded. "If we are really just family, then the acknowledging of Gideon as part of the agreement should have been done years ago and just petty on his brother's part to keep him out like that. So you should do that regardless but I want a favour on top of it all."

The Emperor studied her for a long moment, then said, "I don't want an open-ended favour. Those can be deadly."

"On the level of the favour we are doing for you. A little risk but nothing major." The Emperor actually chuckled. She didn't think he was the one to laugh very often, despite his casual air.

He flicked his hand. "Fine, a small favour. This was more expensive than I thought it would be."

Hara grinned. "Next time it can always be gold."

He shook his head. "Gold is finite. Favours I can give away. The cost is always down the line." The Emperor turned to Gideon. "I see what you see in her. A good choice for your collection."

With that, the Emperor dismissed them. Hara was already down the stairs of the gazebo before she shook off the surreal nature of the whole meeting. Had she really just haggled with the Emperor? Who was now her grandnephew!

Hara turned to Gideon, who was walking beside her. "I need to see a family tree. Just who am I related to now?"

Gideon grinned. "Just about everyone. Why do you think others left me alone even though I wasn't part of the agreement? Harlen is probably the only one of the family who will treat with you much though."

Hara frowned. "Why is that?"

Gideon grinned. "Because Harlen likes you."

She shook her head slowly as her thoughts congealed around the small kernel of horror that she was part of this crazy world of Gideon's and that she had chosen it. She was much better off with being connected to the Emperor and other dragons than to her father. It was for the sake of her Opa that she didn't cut all ties to her family.

Harlen was waiting for them on the path towards the ballroom. He didn't look happy that he had to speak with them. Angel who was sitting on his shoulder was another matter. Angel trilled at her excitement in seeing them and launched into the air. She landed a little awkwardly on Hara's shoulder. Mainly because Hara's shoulders were bare. Angel muttered in frustration as she tangled her claws in Hara's hair to get a grip without scratching Hara beyond repair.

Hara lifted a hand up to the clock work creature until she settled.

Harlen said, "She found me."

Hara smiled at the gruff tone in Harlen's voice. "She is her own creature. I would have thought Janus would have found her before she got bored and wandered off, though. I'm not surprised she got bored with the things we left her. She wanted to come to the ball but we worried she might disrupt things."

Harlen shrugged. Clearly, he didn't care for whatever reason. Hara changed the topic. "The Emperor says he will acknowledge Gideon as part of the original compact you guys made."

Harlen grunted. "Our brother should have done it years ago."

Hara mock fainted at Harlen's admission. Waving a hand to her face. "You actually like Gideon, don't you or are you finally warming up to me."

Harlen's only answer was to say, "You are acceptable for a dragon's collection."

Hara glanced at Gideon, who said, "That is a compliment from him. He is very picky. Even when we had a lot of humans in our collections, he didn't have any."

Harlen said, "They are annoying. They insist on talking. You at least, aren't nearly as annoying as the birds that twitter around court." Harlen tilted his head as he took the two of them. "So you will take the Emperor's offer."

Hara answered, though he hadn't asked it as a question. "Of course. We had intended to when we came here. The Emperor would have lost face if we had declined. But if we decided not to do the favour, we would have not answered the summons. The Emperor could pretend that he never summoned us in that case and save face."

"What are your plans then, to retrieve the girl?" Harlen asked but his tone was bored.

"Well, we will go to the Duke's castle and pretend we are smugglers who are going to help him shift goods. If he is as shifty as implied, then he will look for discreet people. While we are there, we will look around for the girl. She might not be at the castle." Hara answered with a small shake of her head as she thought about the logical thing to do.

"True, he has a few holdings." Harlen agreed.

"But most likely he has her close by at his castle. We won't have long to look but there should be signs she is there. Once we know where she is, we will break her out. Hopefully without destroying too much." Hara was still thinking the problem through.

Harlen looked at them with a creased forehead for a long moment. Eventually he said, "The Emperor would not be disappointed if the Duke was no longer an issue."

Hara wasn't pleased with that. "We are aware of that but we are not assassins. We might be in for some rescuing damsels in distress and causing mayhem but we really don't want to kill anyone."

"You might not have a choice." Harlen's voice was intense.

"We know and that is the risk we will take." Hara knew that every time they took on something like this, that blood being spilt was a possibility. They would just not court violence like some did.

"Will you leave soon?" Harlen asked.

"In the morning." It would be better to leave sooner rather than later. Besides, she was already bored with the life at court.

"Will you return to the dancing?"

Hara looked down at her gown when Harlen asked the question. She was long ready to remove it. "Dancing would be a more appetising activity if I didn't have to wear this get up to achieve it."

Gideon purred, "We can always have private dancing."

Harlen interrupted anything else Gideon was about to say. "I don't wish to know of what you two do in private."

Harlen spun on his heels and left them without even a goodbye.

Hara said, "I think he is warming to me."

"In your dreams, sweetheart. Harlen doesn't warm to anyone. Even his own family."

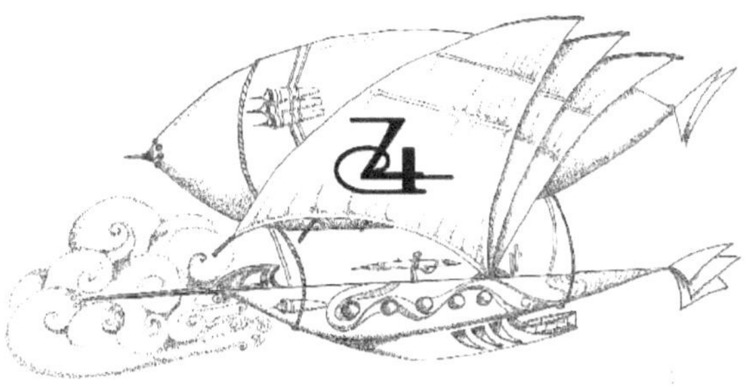

A ngel tittered and warned them that someone was approaching them. Usually it was a woman wanting to catch Gideon's attention but this time it was a young man.

He had blonde hair and a beard manicured to an inch of it's life. His dress was the usual bright foppish extravaganza, which was favoured by the courtiers. He strode up to them and stepped into their path, forcing them to stop and contend with him.

Hara eyed him for a moment. She wasn't used to the courtiers and most had ignored her. The ones who had paid any attention to her were more interested in stealing Angel away and the compliments had been hollow and double edged.

When the fop spoke, he used his hands to speak more than his voice. "You are heading to rescue my bride. I insist you take me along."

Hara raised an eyebrow. If he thought this was a way to ask for a favour, he would need to change his attitude. Even the Emperor had been more polite. Gideon snorted and she realised he was struggling not to laugh. She shook her head at his antics and said to the boy because she realised now he really was only a young man. "Look here. I decide who goes on my ship and who does not. And having someone demand anything from me gives me an itch to use some violence."

It didn't but she wanted to get across to the courtier. He didn't have the power he thought he did. He seemed surprised by her words and stuttered for a moment until he figured out what he was going to say. "But it is my bride you are going to rescue."

Hara turned to Gideon. "Did we even get a name from the Emperor for the groom?"

Gideon shook his head. "I don't think he cared or even knew. He just called him 'boy'."

Hara shrugged. It wasn't like it really mattered. She turned back to the courtier. "Why should I take you? Having the dubious sobriquet of 'boy' from the Emperor implies that you really don't have the clout to make me do anything regardless of your relationship to the girl."

The young man frowned. "You don't know who I am? I am Lord Demetrius Magnus, the third, and my family can trace our line to Charlemagne." He really sounded flabbergasted that anyone would be clueless to his ancestry.

"Really? That is interesting but still doesn't tell me why I should take you along." Hara made sure her voice sounded bored as she didn't want to extend this conversation longer than she had to.

Demetrius looked around and said in a near whisper, "I'm the reason Hermia ran away. I thought that if she got to know me a little, she wouldn't think I wasn't such a bad match. But if you rescue her and take her home to her family, the problem of before will still remain. She still won't want to marry me."

Hara studied him for a long moment. The boy actually had a point. Though the Emperor really hadn't cared if the marriage went forward, it was still a good match, according to the Empress and the girl wouldn't have to be worried about being kidnapped by the Duke. In all, it really wasn't her problem but she knew the Emperor would be happier if there were fewer loose ends at the end of the mission. He would certainly be more amenable to any favour she asked for.

Hara's eyes drifted over his clothes and the manicured beard. "You can't come looking like that. Everyone will know that you're a lord and the whole point of this mission is that, on paper, Gideon and I are complete unknowns."

Demetrius' hand went to the collar of his coat. "I wouldn't have to wear rags, would I?"

Hara shook her head. "Just normal clothes."

He sniffed. "These are normal clothes."

Hara resisted the urge to roll her eyes and she had to consciously ignore Gideon's snickers as she said, "Just ask your valet to dress you up as a servant when you board the ship tomorrow morning and I'll get Alice to set you up with a proper outfit."

Demetrius' eyes gleamed. "Will it be a pirate outfit?"

Gideon lost the battle with his laughter and had to lean against the wall as he struggled to breathe past the muffled gaffs of laughter. Hara turned a quick glare in Gideon's direction. She knew part of the laughter was directed at her but there was no point in arguing it over with Gideon in the presence of the young nobleman.

Instead, she turned to Demetrius. "No, not a bloody pirate's outfit. We're a merchant vessel who does special deliveries."

Demetrius' eyes went wide. "You are smugglers then?"

Well, they had been smugglers for the last few months as with the stigma of pirate over their head they hadn't been able to take a legitimate cargo. Though stinting the government on tax wasn't going to make her lose any sleep at night.

Gideon laughed louder and was on the floor now. Her shoulders stiff, she answered curtly, "Just be there tomorrow morning or we'll leave without you. We can get the girl without you, but you need us to get to the girl." She turned to Gideon. "You better get your arse off that floor or I'm coming over to kick you."

He got up to his knees and looked at her with glistening eyes. "You do know you will never lose the notoriety, Hara? You will always be a pirate to the Empire and to the Roshians and that means pretty much the entire world."

Hara felt perverse. "Maybe we will go to Han then. They are no friend to the Empire or to the Roshians. I shouldn't have a name there."

Gideon got to his feet. "Promise?"

She frowned, confused by the question. "Promise what?"

He lightly touched her cheek. His face very serious now. Obviously, whatever he was asking of her was important enough to chase away any of his mirth. "Promise me that we will go to Han. They won't know what to do with you."

She smacked him on his shoulder. "Stop teasing me."

He shook his head as he rubbed where she had hit him. "No, I love it when you turn people's worlds upside down."

Gideon nodded his head in the direction of where Demetrius had gone. "He will return to court a very different man after he has spent some time with you. I have seen it with the others and with myself and I want to see how you can change the Han who have been set in their ways since before even the dragons came to this planet.”

“I’m not trouble, you know. It just seems to follow me around.” Hara wasn’t sure if she was flattered or aghast that she changed people in his view.

Gideon shrugged. “Trouble? No, but change? Yes. Change can be chaos or it can create something beautiful. And with you, I think even the chaos is beautiful.”

Hara looked at him from the corner of her eye as they walked towards their room. She wasn’t sure if he was being serious but then he seemed solemn and Gideon wasn’t much for seriousness in any case. They came to their suite. It had a sitting room and a bedroom.

There was something unspoken between them that made sharing a room easy. Hara contemplated talking to him about his tendency to end up in her bed on a regular basis but she was worried that if they ever had that conversation he might convince her she was actually ready for more from their relationship.

It was an unfounded fear as Gideon hadn’t pressured her into anything and Hara was mostly sure she was ready, anyway. It was only fear holding her back at this stage. Fear that her demons would get between the two of them and mess up what they had.

Angel glided off Hara’s shoulder when they entered the room and found herself a place to sleep. Janus was lying on the couch. He was snoring softly. Gideon kicked his leg and he stumbled to his feet, babbling until he got his bearings. When Janus looked around and saw Angel curled up and asleep, he pointed an accusing finger at her but eventually just sighed and turned back to them. “So how did the visit with the Emperor go?”

Hara answered, "Surprisingly well. We just have to collect a runaway bride and lug a moping groom along the way."

Janus snorted with laughter. "Well, better you than me." He yawned and headed towards the door with a small wave. "I'll make sure to see you off in the morning."

"You better. The last time I left, you merely made a rude gesture at me as I was riding away," Gideon accused him.

Janus frowned as he tried to recollect the event, then grinned warmly. "Oh, yeah, that was because you had left me saddled with Lady Boshin."

Gideon laughed. "Oh, Lady Boshin. She really could talk."

"It was the hands that were the problem." Janus waved another goodbye and left the room.

Gideon went to the door to close it behind him and leant against it as he looked at her.

Hara tried to reach around for the laces at the back of her dress. She couldn't wait long enough to get out to call for a servant. She jumped when Gideon's hands brushed away her fingers and he started undoing the laces. Hara could have called for the servant who had helped her into the contraption in the first place but she liked the thrill that went down her spine, the light touch of Gideon's hands. Gideon liked to invade her space but he had drawn a line in the sand and always left when she was getting naked or changing.

Gideon pushed the dress off so it pooled at her feet. He asked, "Better."

"Much." She turned and started picking up all the petticoats. Gideon caught her hands and took the dress out of them and threw it onto a chair.

He then whirled her around. "We can dance here. You don't have the dress on anymore."

She huffed. "And not much else."

"I like that." She looked into his eyes but he didn't move his hands away from the modest touch on her waist and hand.

Hara asked, "Gideon, what do you see in me? I'm a mess. I can't trust men because of the rat bag my father is. Why do you insist on being—well—decent?"

Gideon took her through another whirl and said after some thought, "Your fear of trusting men only means you were free when I found you. That was never a deterrent. You are smart and clever. Yes, they are different things. But you are also kind. You rescued me from Roshian Revolutionaries, even though you had no idea if I was a good person or not. It is that kindness that draws me to you. The human race is capable of such honour and it shines from you, unlike others."

Hara stopped dancing and pulled Gideon to a stop. He frowned at her. But she didn't let him wonder for long. She leant forward and kissed him. It was light and fleeting but Gideon pulled her back.

This time, the kiss was anything but light. She could feel the fierce need in Gideon. It would have frightened her before but it didn't this night. He didn't move his hands. If he did, she would have skittered away. But after a long moment, he pulled back.

He searched her eyes. "Not yet. Almost, but not yet."

Hara had to agree with him as she forced her heart to settle down. She was thrilled by the unknown he was offering but she was still contemplating if the fall was worth it. Especially as she had to trust him to catch her.

Janus looked tired as if he had headed back to the ball after he had left them the night before. He was even wearing the same clothes he had worn the night before as he stood to give them a farewell.

He glared blurringly at Gideon. "I hope this is worth it."

Gideon clapped him on the back. "Probably not. But I'm glad you are here. There are very few at court who would even care if I keeled over and died let alone leave court."

Hara said as she came up behind Gideon, "The women would care."

Janus snorted but Gideon did not look amused. He accused her. "Are you two ganging up on me?"

Janus said sweetly, "Would never even dream of it. We have been friends since before we even came to this planet. I would be a right bastard to match up with a human to gang up on you. Now if I can convince her to—"

Gideon put up his hand to interrupt anything else Janus was going to say. Gideon's face became serious. "All jokes aside, Janus. You look after yourself. You might see more of me now that I've stopped sulking."

Hara asked, interested, "Sulking?"

Gideon answered, "That was what he accused me of when I left Court the last time. He wasn't wrong, though. I was disillusioned with the world and I was sulking. It took you to make me realise there was still fun to be had."

Hara grinned. "Mayhem maybe. You say your goodbyes. I got to make sure everything is stored away." She headed towards the airship where Murphy shifted a trunk onto the lift.

Gideon came to stand next to her and she asked, "So quickly?"

Gideon shrugged. "We were never ones for long goodbyes."

Hara looked at him carefully for a long moment. Gideon didn't have many friends, human or dragon. She had certainly not found one who knew Gideon so well. She envied him that connection. Dressing up as a boy and conning people made it difficult for her to make childhood friends. Now that she was no longer hiding, she had a responsibility to people and that made it difficult to make friends.

She liked the people on the Blazing Blunderbuss but they weren't quite friends either. Gideon was the only one she would class as a friend and her feelings for him were all jumbled up to the point where it was painful to examine them so mostly she left them alone.

Demetrius waited for them below the airship. Hara hadn't seen him while the lift was down. His dress was rather ridiculous as it was all mismatched and either a size too big or too small. Hara raised an eyebrow as she took him in. He stood proud and didn't seem to care how he looked. She hoped that pride didn't come back to bite him later.

Hara whistled and the lift came down. Alice was on the platform and eyed the young Demetrius with a suspicious eye.

Hara said, "This is the young groom, Demetrius."

Alice raised her own eyebrows at the revelation. "Groom? As in horses or brides?"

"The girl we are going to rescue is his bride but keep that to yourself. As far as anyone knows, Demetrius is a new crew member. You have anything for him to wear?"

Alice looked Demetrius up and down. "I'll find something because he certainly isn't very convincing the way he looks now."

Alice waved for Demetrius to follow her onto the platform. When they were all on, Alice said, "We have a passenger. He is flexible about his time frame as he wants to head out of the Empire and he doesn't care when or even where."

Hara said, "We are going near the border. He might be happy to go that far."

If not, it wouldn't take much to take him over the border. Alice locked in the platform when the lift reached the deck and tugged on Demetrius' arm. "Come boy. We better get you kitted out before the rest hurt themselves, laughing at the sight of you."

Their new passenger was sitting in the mess when Hara and Gideon arrived. He was a short man with a balding pate. He was also the kind that fidgeted. He had piled up small pieces of paper on the table and was trying to lay a paper roof on the small structure. When they entered and opened the door, a gust of wind made his structure wobble.

He glanced up to look at them before he returned to completing his structure. He said conversationally, "I take it you are the Captain."

Hara took a seat. "Captain Hara. And you are?"

He finished and looked up and offered his hand. "Puck is the name. I'm heading out of the Empire and I was looking for a ride that would keep me safe and be a little interesting."

"Ah, is there someone after you." That would explain why he was flexible and not scared that he was amongst ex-pirates.

He shrugged. "No one in particular." He tapped his temple. "But people have wanted what is in here before and I won't be surprised if they try again."

She thought he was actually crazy but he was a paying passenger so she would just avoid him. Hara got up and saw the look Gideon was giving the new passenger. Gideon was a mathematician, he wasn't a soldier but he looked deadly at that moment.

Hara motioned for him to follow her as she left. Once they were far enough away that Puck wouldn't hear them, Hara asked, "Do you know him?"

"No, but I know of him. He is an engineer like you but he makes creatures like Angel. His creatures, though, don't have the same sentience as Angel. But he has a reputation for causing mischief." Gideon's protective nature always surprised Hara, as people in her life were the kind to use her rather than protect her. Even her Opa, who always let her father take her off to god knows where for his cons, hadn't protected her like Gideon did. Without smothering her at the same time like Talen was trying to do.

"Oh?" Last summer, they had met a scientist who had been making poisons to kill dragons. He hadn't been malicious though, just curious and they had managed to turn his greed for a lab to make him change his purpose. Hara wondered if this engineer was similar.

<hr>

Hermia found a spot in the library that was quiet and had enough sun that she could read well into the afternoon. It was tucked away behind a set of shelves. The back of the shelves was a beautiful wood carved panel. A good idea, for the sun would have bleached the colour out of any artwork or the spines of the books.

Someone had thought it was a suitable spot for reading as they had put a big comfy chair and a small brazier. She had never seen Duke Lysander here so she doubted he had been the one to set it up as a reading spot.

Hermia was so absorbed by the book she didn't hear the people enter the room. It was only when one snapped. "It is dangerous."

The woman's voice had a slight Roshian accent so she wasn't a local, though Rosha wasn't too far away from the way a bird flew. It was the woman who had warned her the first night she had been here.

Hermia was about to stick her head around to see who the strange woman was when she heard Duke Lysander drawl, "You are too cautious, my dear. Fortune favours the bold, Helena."

Helena, the woman obviously, growled back, "You are going to throw away everything we have done for this girl. She is related to the Emperor. He will not allow you to marry her without his permission. You will declare war on the throne if you do that."

Lysander didn't seem concerned at all. "I have married before someone the Emperor didn't want me to marry. I had her disappear and still he did nothing. The Emperor has no teeth. He will do nothing now. Besides, if he takes offence, it just means my bid for the throne will move forward a little."

Hermia's heart grew cold and she was pale as she held her breath, scared they would hear the beating of her heart and realise she was there. Hermia knew she was the girl they spoke of as her aunt on her mother's side had married the Emperor. If Hermia had known the plan was to force her into another marriage, she would never have come here.

The woman, Helena, continued, "You are brash, Lysander. The Emperor might seem weak but he has the backing of the dragons and you will not be able to dismiss them so easily."

Their voices were getting softer as they walked out of the library. Hermia struggled to pick up what Lysander said but only caught the word 'mechanicals'.

Once they had left, Hermia allowed herself to breathe deeply. There had been spots in her eyes as she had been breathing so shallowly in fear that they would hear her.

She wanted to rush out and get as far as she could but she knew that since she walked in here, she wouldn't be allowed to leave. Now that she knew Lysander wanted her for political power, she could see her appeal to him. Her land was where the pass went between the Empire and to the rest of the world in this corner of the world. He could move in troops by land and by air. Her link to the throne would also help him as once he killed the Emperor, there was no one else with a clearer path to the throne except her brothers.

Hermia hated being used as a pawn and she had been silly enough to think someone would help her out of the goodness of their hearts. She wouldn't make that mistake again. Surely she could find some way out of the castle and out of the Duke's clutches.

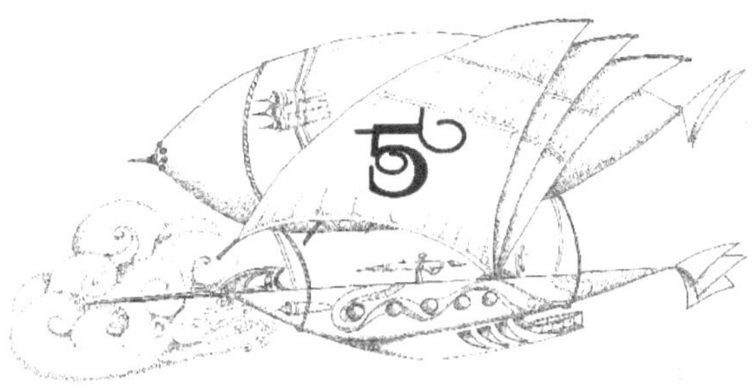

Demetrius followed the girl called Alice to a small room. He looked around. "Is this for the servants?"

Alice huffed. "You can sleep here or out on the deck. It is your choice. I left some clothes for you in the drawers. They are Liam's but they should fit you. Drop your things and I'll show you the rest of the ship."

Demetrius inspected the room. There was a small bed with high sides. Underneath there were drawers. A small table and stool were bolted to the wall and the floor, respectively. Otherwise, there was nothing else in the room.

Demetrius said, "Surely there is a bigger room than this. The airship is rather large."

"Yes, and that is to hold cargo. The only room which is bigger is the Captain's."

Demetrius thought out loud, "I wonder if the–"

Alice snapped. "You will not oust the Captain from her room. You are here only as a favour. You will work as part of the crew and you will be treated as crew. Here you are not a lord. Here you are nothing but another crew member under the Captain's command."

Demetrius's hackles rose at the tone of the woman's voice. "And who are you to speak to me like that?"

Alice stepped in close to him and said in a calm voice, "I'm the first mate and you will listen to me like the rest of the crew has to."

Demetrius stepped back first. Alice nodded like his retreat was the right response. She turned. "Hurry up. I don't have all day."

Demetrius quickly dropped his bag and followed Alice; no, the first mate, as she led the way through the narrow corridors of the Blazing Blunderbuss. He had to skip to keep up.

"I thought the dragon would be first mate," He said curious.

Alice didn't look back as she answered, "You would have thought wrong. Gideon is the Captain's mate but he does nothing on the ship. Unless we need a dragon. It helps to chase off pirates when we have a dragon on board."

Demetrius couldn't argue with that but he would have thought that Gideon would have been in charge of everything on the ship considering that Hara was in his collection. He had always found dragons to be obsessed with controlling things. If Alice thought he was arrogant for wanting a bigger room, she would be shocked with the dragons who orbited the Emperor's court.

Alice stepped aside and waved for Demetrius to enter the room. Inside was a long table and a galley-style kitchen down one side of the room. There were two men already sitting at the table but at opposite ends.

Alice followed him into the room. "This is our gunner, Murphy."

The muscle-bound man at one end of the table waved a fork in the air as a greeting, but he was concentrating on his food rather than on greeting the new crew member.

Alice motioned to the other man. "This is a paying passenger. His name is Puck. You are to treat him with respect."

The last of those words were said with a lot of force. What did Alice expect? For him to insult the man? Demetrius had a witty retort on his lips but swallowed it. Instead, he glared at Alice.

A shadow just behind Demetrius' shoulder made him flinch. A small metal dragon flew over his head into the room. It landed on the table and chortled to the muscled man, Murphy. Murphy offered the clockwork creature a bowl of metal nuts. The small dragon then collected out the nuts and started piling them in sets on the table.

The man, Puck, seemed intrigued by the dragon and its simple task.

Puck asked, "Who is this divine creature?"

Alice huffed. "None of your business."

Murphy swallowed a mouthful to say, "Yeah, better keep away from her. The last person to take an interest in the boss's dragon got left in Rosh."

Alice threatened mockingly, "If someone bother's Angel here, I can assure you that the captain will detach your dragon and leave it in Rosh."

Demetrius was surprised to see that the passenger wasn't intimidated by this threat. Demetrius almost questioned Alice on the wisdom of threatening their passenger just after she had instructed him to be on his best behaviour.

⬥⎯⎯⎯⎯⎯⎯⎯⬥

Demetrius was woken by a slight sound. The hum of the engines was almost comforting in the background but he had heard something that scraped. He got to his feet and listened at the door. He heard the scrape again.

Cautiously, he opened the door. He wasn't sure what he would find outside his room. It was late and most of the crew was in bed. Just the night watch was awake.

Demetrius was surprised to see the passenger, Puck, just outside his door. The man had his back turned to Demetrius. Puck was crouched over and working on something on the opposite wall of the corridor by the Captain's door.

Demetrius cleared his throat and the passenger, Puck, jumped and spun around in surprise. Demetrius asked, "What are you about, Puck? Nothing sinister, eh?"

Puck flashed a grin. "Hardly. I dropped something and I'm trying to find it. I know I dropped it in this corridor but it is so blasted small it is taking a while to find it."

That didn't explain the scraping sound but it wasn't Demetrius' place to interrogate the man. He might mention it to the Captain in the morning, though he thought the Captain might already realise that their passenger was a weird one. Demetrius thought when he went on this adventure it would be more interesting than listening to engineers debating the merits of clockwork creatures and automata over supper. The only person who had appeared interesting, with weapons strapped to his body, had turned out to be a dim-witted gun-happy man.

Demetrius' parents would not be pleased when they heard he had come along to rescue Hermia. They had been the driving force behind him marrying Hermia. If she hadn't run off, he would have run off himself. He wasn't interested in marrying someone he didn't know. He had told Hara the truth when he said he wanted to come along so the two of them could actually get to know each other. Demetrius might have defied his parents by coming on this airship but he knew when he returned they would put a huge amount of pressure on him to marry Hermia and he wanted to be sure that he could actually like her when he caved.

Demetrius asked, "You want a hand to look for your missing… whatever it is you are missing?"

Puck waved it off. "I might wait for the morning when the light is better. But thank you for the offer."

Puck sauntered off towards his room and Demetrius shrugged and returned to his own bed. He had other things to worry about besides an eccentric engineer.

<hr>

The bridge was quiet when Hara came up for her watch. Alice was still at the helm. Alice looked tired but she soon could head to her own bunk. Hara asked, "Everything shipshape?"

"Yeah," Alice said warily.

Alice rubbed her face and Hara asked, "You alright?"

Alice nodded. "Just we could do with more crew."

A ship this size often had a dozen crew members. There wasn't much Hara could do about it in the meantime. While they were still classed as ex-pirates, they only attracted the shady or the downright criminal. She had been contemplating automating much of the ship but that would take money and time. Neither one of the abundant while they were running from authorities.

Hara asked, "How is Demetrius doing?"

"If he can get the stick out of his arse, he will be all right." Hara laughed. Alice wasn't one to use vulgar language so she knew she had strong opinions on the young nobleman. Hara wasn't surprised by that. Hara had developed her own strong opinions of noblemen and they were still very much accurate.

It had only been Gideon that had made her rethink some of her assumptions.

Hara asked, "Not pining for him to warm your bed, then?"

Alice snorted. "Hardly, though I do think I might like to have a man. I see the way you are with Gideon. It isn't even about the heat between the two of you. It would be nice to have someone care about me. Is all. You aren't going to ask me if I could like anyone already on board?"

Hara shook her head. "Who is there to choose from? Henry is a bit old for you. Liam is too young. Murphy is not your match brain wise."

Alice raised an eyebrow. "What about Talen? You know he has tried to get his way into my bed?"

Hara wrinkled her nose. "Definitely not Talen. He is a scoundrel. He doesn't have a moral bone in his body. And he is even older than Henry."

Alice frowned. "Then why do you have him on board. I know he annoys Gideon. Talen has been trying to get between the two of you from the beginning."

"Because Talen is actually trying to figure out how to go the straight and narrow. It is alien to him so he needs help. When he figures out that why he is here, he'll leave Gideon alone. He isn't in love with me but he still needs me and he is worried that Gideon will stop me from helping him."

Alice shook her head. "So if he is the last option, there really is no option on this ship for me."

Hara had to agree with her. But as long as Alice travelled with them, they were unlikely to come across someone like Gideon for Alice.

Hara took her position at the helm. "I swear we will only take on passengers who are kind and handsome and once we have our pardon, I'll hire young virile men who can keep you company."

Alice snorted with laughter but there was a seriousness to the whole conversation that neither of them could deny. It would be difficult for Alice. In the world they lived in, people had a set view of what women were supposed to be like and how they should act.

Hara knew better than anyone how those views could make a woman feel stifled. Alice was a bright woman who had taken to being first mate like a fish to water. Surely Hara could do her bit and see if she could play matchmaker for the girl.

Hara had a better idea. She would put Gideon on it. He had a good sense of people and what made them good people. Anyone he found for Alice would be a decent fellow and they would see how things went from there.

<hr>

Hara came to stand by Gideon, who was in his favourite spot on the bridge, a chair that looked through the large windows at the front.

She asked, "What do you see?"

He had better eyesight than her in any of his forms. "He has stripped the land."

Hara leaned over to see down onto the land. It was all cultivated and the land torn from farming for more people than the Duchy could reasonably hold. He must be selling the excess. Hara wondered what he would need the money for.

The castle itself came into view and Gideon said, "If you want to make an entrance, cut the engines soon and bank left. Hard."

Hara gave the order to Alice, who was at the helm. The Blazing Blunderbuss skidded across the sky. Hara wasn't worried, though everyone on the bridge was holding on as they tipped precariously. Gideon had been in the air all his life and he knew the specs for the ship so he could make calculations in his head.

The Blazing Blunderbuss came to a rocky stop. Hara looked out of the window and saw that they were above the wall of the castle. Several soldiers were pointing weapons at them but they didn't dare shoot. If they clipped the envelope, they might cause an explosion and even if they didn't and brought the airship down, it would take out the whole east tower.

Hara pursed her lips, impressed by how close Gideon's calculations had brought them. She turned and gave orders to Liam to secure them. She went out to the deck and called down to the soldiers, "We are here to see the Duke. We have a business proposition for him."

One soldier peeled off and dashed down the stairs. They would hear soon enough if they were permitted to stay. Hara hoped the fancy flying would convince the Duke that they were the kind of flyers that he needed to move his goods. Considering the way the Duke had stripped his land, she knew he would have a lot to move.

A woman came out. She had red hair in a braid and wore a sumptuous velvet gown, though Hara could imagine her in similar clothes as her own of leather breeches. The woman studied them with a hand on her waist. "What brings you all here?"

Her Roshian accent was subtle, telling Hara that the woman had been living outside of Rosh for a while. But Hara had been listening to a lot of Roshian accents recently and knew that was the woman's origins. Curious to have a Roshian woman in the Empire questioning them for the Duke.

Hara understood now the Emperor's concerns. Hara called down, "We heard you might need an airship to move cargo and we are the best. Do you think we can come down and talk like civilised people?"

The Roshian woman studied them with narrowed eyes but eventually nodded her head. Hara descended the rope ladder with Gideon. The others waited above.

The Roshian woman eyed the two of them. "Who are you?"

Hara offered a hand which the woman ignored but Hara simply shrugged it off. "I am Captain Hara and this is my mate Gideon."

The woman looked at Gideon. "What are you?"

Gideon smiled with his teeth before he answered, "I'm a mathematician." He motioned to the ship. "How do you think we knew when to cut the engines to make a move like that?"

The Roshian woman shook her head, clearly expecting another answer. Instead, she introduced herself. "I am Helena. The Duke says you may stay for the night and then you will leave in the morning." The usual guesting laws.

Hara grinned. "Perfect. We will have him convinced before supper that we are the ones he needs."

Hara whistled and Alice sent the lift down with the others. They had decided that most of them would go into the castle just in case Hara needed the muscle. But Alice along with Henry and their passenger Puck would remain on the airship to help them escape when they needed to. Single file, the crew of Blazing Blunderbuss followed Helena into the castle and off the wall.

Gideon ran his hand over the wall and said to himself, "Interesting."

Hara wondered if it was an 'interesting' he could share in a mixed crowd or whether she would have to wait until they were private. Gideon obviously thought it was safe to share as he turned to her. "The walls are very thick. Very thick." He emphasised the last sentence.

Helena glanced over her shoulder. "The castle which was here before didn't suit the Duke. He has made some improvements since his wife's death." Helena glanced at Gideon and added in a reverent voice, "Most people don't even notice."

Gideon flashed Helena a grin. "I told you I'm good with numbers."

Helena lowered her lashes. "I'm sure that isn't the only thing you are good at."

Hara let a smirk touch her lips. It seemed that no matter where they went, people would flirt with Gideon.

Hara put the girl out of her misery. "He is taken." Helena looked at Hara and raised an eyebrow in question so Hara answered, "Yes, he is mine."

Gideon corrected her. "Actually, she is mine. We are still negotiating about me being hers but I have high hopes it will be agreed upon soon."

Hara blushed. She knew what Gideon was talking about and it wasn't just about collections. It was about sharing his bed.

Hara hissed at Gideon. "Is there a reason you are sharing this information with strangers?"

Gideon shrugged but otherwise didn't answer. Helena brought them into a large hall where the Duke was draped over an elaborate throne. When he saw Gideon, though, he quickly got to his feet. He stalked towards the crew and Gideon.

Duke Lysander was a tall man with striking features. He wore black with a white blousy shirt. He studied

Gideon as he approached. "What brings such interesting people to my door?"

Hara knew she needed to set the tone so said crisply, "Money. We heard you need things moved and you pay well for a diverse crew."

The Duke turned his attention to her. He stalked towards her like a panther. He caught Hara's hands and brought them up to his lips, one hand at a time.

He kissed the knuckles of one hand as he said, "Diverse? Certainly beauty is part of what makes your crew diverse."

Murphy smacked Liam on the arm. "See, the Duke also thinks you are cute."

Talen snapped. "Shush. He must be lying, as no one would think you are cute, Murphy, and he included the whole crew."

Murphy looked offended. "Excuse me. I was once sold as a sex slave. They said I had a stunning physique." He demonstrated by flexing his muscles.

The Duke looked confused at the debate amongst Hara's crew so she took his hands and drew him away. Gideon could make sure the rest didn't get into trouble. "Why don't we discuss this in private, my lord? I'm sure we could come to some accommodation."

The Duke thread her hand through the crook of his arm and flashed her a brilliant smile. "I think that is a marvellous idea, my flower."

Hara wanted to gag. The Duke took her to a study and released her to pour a drink. He motioned with the brandy bottle for her to take a seat. Playing to her part, she sat on the edge of the table and picked up something random.

She said casually, "You have a nice place here. I heard the missus gave it to you when she started pushing up daisies."

"Over two years now. She would have been proud of what I have made of her former home. But I don't really want to speak of deceased spouses. Tell me about the dragon that is with you." He finished pouring his drink.

"Gideon? What is there to tell? He is annoying but he is useful. I can guarantee you won't have to worry about pirates or anyone else messing with your cargo. That is the special extras that only my crew can offer and worth every penny." Hara hated sometimes when she used her acting skills she had learnt at her father's knee.

The Duke gave her a glass of brandy and asked, "Will the dragon mind if he shared you?" Over his dead body.

Hara was in desperate need for a shower. She didn't understand how he had convinced a naive girl that he was safe enough to find refuge with. "What he doesn't know won't hurt him." Hara purred.

The Duke put his hand over her hand, which held her glass. "Shall we seal our deal now or later?"

Hara smiled flirtatiously but inside she was thinking of ways to gouge out his eyes. "Tonight after everyone is asleep. I will come to your room."

The Duke leant down to give her a kiss but at the last moment she turned her head so he kissed her cheek.

When he pulled back and frowned at her evasion, she said, "Tonight. I want you to be patient and trust me, it will be worth it." Hara reached out and ran a hand over his chest. She hopped off the table. "Now let us set in writing the deal. I'm sure you will want us to get to work straight away."

The Duke eyed her for a long while. "I will have my man of affairs see to it. Have dinner with us tonight and it should be ready when you come to see me tonight."

"Tonight." She even batted her eyelashes. Mostly because she needed to hide the shudder of disgust that ran down her spine.

When Hara left the study to find the others, she found Helena had taken them to their rooms. Only Gideon was waiting for her. She rushed over to him and tugged on his hand to take them somewhere private. She shuddered as she thought of the Duke.

When she looked at Gideon, he had a strange look on his face.

Hara asked, "Are you alright?"

Gideon asked, "Did he flirt with you?"

"Outrageously. He expects me to warm his bed in order to get the shipping deal. How crass?"

"Do you feel like I do when the noble women flirt with me?"

An interesting question. She hadn't liked it when the noblewomen had flirted with him back at the court but she had known he wouldn't do anything about it. He had lived a very long time. He had once lived at court as well and he had decided that she was interesting enough to add to his collection. She didn't think the noble women had anything that was new or interesting to him.

She answered cautiously, "Yes."

He pulled her close against his body. "Then I'll make sure the servants send up a bath to your room."

He was right. She felt the urge to scrub every inch of skin the man had touched. It also made her realise that the noble women really didn't hold any appeal for him.

Hara let herself settle against his chest. "We have to play nice for supper tonight. You think you can do that?"

"Yes. As doing anything else will put us in danger."

She liked that he was practical like that. She asked, worried, "You don't mind waiting for me to be ready?"

"I'm a dragon. I have waited this long for you. Months and weeks are a mere drop in the ocean of time I have already lived. I can wait." He said with enough fervour that she knew he was telling the truth.

Hara took in a deep breath with relief. She realised Gideon smelt different to every other man she had been close to. He smelt pleasant but she couldn't put her finger on what made his scent different. It just was. She could stay there in his arms all night.

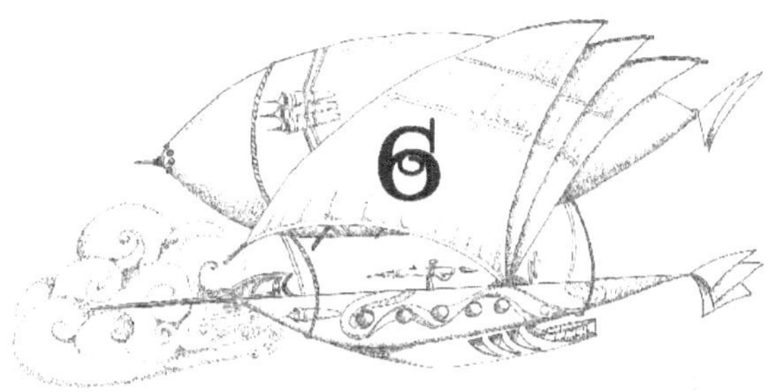

The Duke certainly knew how to put on a spread. Hara filled her plate and winked at the Duke as she stuffed her face. She was hoping she disgusted him a little bit so he would change his mind about wanting her in his bed. Not that she planned to get near his bed. The Duke kept his face bland as he tipped his glass in her direction.

Gideon asked, "You have a lovely place here. How did you come to live here?"

The Duke narrowed his eyes. "The castle belonged to my late wife. She had such grand dreams for its glory but died before it could come to pass."

Hara wanted to roll her eyes. Could he not be more cliché of a villain? He gloated in such lofty tones.

"Oh, your wife has passed on? Is Helena, your new bride? Congratulations," Gideon asked in a voice overly cheerful as he turned to wink at Helena. She ignored the whole interaction and continued to eat.

The Duke had been taking a sip of his wine and he choked on it. He glared at Gideon. "No, Helena is merely a companion."

Murphy, further down the table, snorted. "Companion? I bet she does more than keep you company."

Liam elbowed Murphy and he glared at the boy. Hara decided she would say something before Murphy messed it up. "Do you have a new bride, then? Is she here?"

"No, alas, I have a broken heart and it would need to be someone of great beauty and wealth to get through to my broken heart." The Duke eyed Hara suggestively as he spoke.

There was some snickering but when Hara glared at the others, they stopped. But she couldn't see who it had been.

Liam said, "You have some fascinating gadgets. Do you make them yourself?"

Thank goodness for that boy. He knew the right thing to say to settle the mood. The Duke sipped his wine magnanimously. "I employ only the best but that is not where my skills lie. I have vision but not the hands to bring that vision to fruition."

Liam seemed disappointed and when Hara looked his way, he explained, "He had a small automaton in the bathrooms."

Murphy piped in. "Oh, yeah, cool little thing but nothing compared to Angel."

Angel was back on the Blazing Blunderbuss. There was no way Hara was going to bring her into enemy territory while they didn't know the enemy's strength. But Hara wouldn't be surprised if she popped up later. There was only so much Alice and Henry could do to keep the small dragon busy.

Liam said, "It scared the bejeebus out of Demetrius."

The Duke said casually, "Demetrius. An interesting name. Since we were talking of brides, I wondered if you had your own bride. Someone young and handsome as you deserve a good woman."

Hara looked at the Duke. Surely he didn't know. They had come straight from the court and no one there had known besides the Emperor what their mission was.

Hara said for Demetrius, "Don't mind Demetrius. He is shy."

That had everyone raising their eyebrows. But Demetrius wisely kept his mouth shut. No one would believe he was truly shy but the conversation around the table turned in another direction. Hara had the feeling that this was only the quiet before the storm.

<hr>

Hara shushed Gideon when he stumbled into a suit of armour which stood on the corner of the corridor. He looked at her while he held the suit to stop it from making any more noise.

Hara whispered, "We are supposed to be quiet. Even Angel has managed to be quiet."

Angel raised her head from Hara's shoulder. Almost to say, "Yeah, Gideon, quiet."

Gideon moved away from the suit of armour and it remained standing so he skipped to follow Hara. They were searching the lower levels of the castle for the missing bride. They had assumed since Hermia hadn't been at dinner that she was probably being kept locked away. And where better to lock someone away in a castle than in a dungeon.

So far, they hadn't found a dungeon or Hermia. They had found all sorts of stores, from food to parts for machines. But no sign of a runaway bride. What they had found as well were a lot of soldiers. There had been soldiers posted on all the stairs and in some corridors.

Gideon asked, "Shouldn't we be looking where there are a lot of soldiers rather than less?"

Hara shook her head. "We can't risk being caught. Maybe later tonight, when the castle is quieter."

Gideon said, "But later you are supposed to be entertaining the Duke." It was clear from his tone he didn't like the idea of her with the Duke.

Hara frowned. She wasn't keen to entertain the Duke either. "Let us look down here first, then we will look upstairs. Hopefully, we can avoid the soldiers."

Gideon said, "If we meet up with the soldiers, then we can pretend we are engaged in something illicit." He wriggled his eyebrows suggestively.

Hara wrinkled her nose. "I don't think people really believe that. I brought some of my tools that can deal with any of the soldiers but it will mean our cover will be blown and we'll have to shoot our way out."

Gideon clapped his hands silently in mock excitement. "Ooh, some fun. Let's head upstairs right away."

Hara shook her head at Gideon's factitious tone. Hara pushed open the next door. The space beyond was dark but it felt bigger than the other rooms so Hara risked a light. The small flame didn't illuminate much of the room but it was clear that it was filled with large objects. Hara squinted to make out the shapes.

Gideon gave her the clue she needed when he said, "They look like giants."

"They are automata. I've never seen ones this big, though," Hara said in a tone of awe.

Hara looked around and saw that the automata were still being put together as most of the guts of the machines were laid out on long tables which lined the walls.

Gideon asked, "What would someone do with machines this big?"

"Nothing good," Hara said seriously.

Gideon asked, "Do you think he would keep Hermia here along with his machines?"

"Probably not. But let us check out the rest of the castle." Hara was worried that Hermia wasn't even here and that their searching was for nothing.

"What are you going to do about the Duke?" Gideon asked what seemed a simple question but she knew Gideon seriously wanted to know the answer.

"Stand him up, of course." She looked at Gideon to see what he thought of that. He cleverly didn't say anything more. Did he seriously think she would sleep with a man just to keep their cover?

⸺⸺⸺⸺⸺⸺⸺⸺⸺⸺

Hermia wasn't surprised when the Duke sent a note and suggested that she stay in her room for her meal. She took most of them alone in any case but she had seen the airship make a spectacular entrance on the wall of the castle when she had been outside for some fresh air.

Now there were twice as many soldiers on all the floors and at all the stairs. To get to where she could see who was visiting had meant ducking and hiding from several soldiers. Hermia was now crouched amongst old tapestries stored above the hall on a mezzanine floor.

The room looked huge, with a tiny table in the middle to accommodate the guests. The Duke was glaring at the people at his table. They, in turn, seemed oblivious to the look. Helena, on the other hand, looked almost bored with the whole thing and paid more attention to her food than to the conversation that was happening around her. Not that the conversation was anything more captivating than young men teasing each other.

There was one young man who kept very quiet at the end of the table. He didn't look as rugged as the others and he used his fork correctly. She didn't think smugglers and ruffians would be taught their manners.

There was one who didn't touch his food at all. He sat with his hands clasped on the table in front of him and he watched the Duke with sharp eyes. Eyes that were the colour of a dragon's.

Hermia had grown up around dragons and hybrids. She knew what a dragon looked like when he was in a human form. Her heart leapt. Almost all the dragons worked for the Emperor. Surely he was here to rescue her. After all, her aunt was the empress.

But she couldn't wander down to dinner now. The Duke would realise that she wasn't complacent and throw her into a dungeon or something. She had to be more subtle about it and that meant she would have to wait. She couldn't wait here and the conversation wasn't anything interesting so she quietly crawled away from the edge of the balcony.

She returned to her room in time for Helena to check on her. Hermia pretended to be reading a book and the woman just nodded in Hermia's direction before leaving her alone. Once Helena left, Hermia sneaked out again.

Hermia had discovered that the thick walls of the castle hid passages. The Duke must have been paranoid as he hadn't informed his soldiers about the passages as they were not at the exits or within as she made her way to the room where the dragon was staying. There was no light under his door and she waited.

Hermia dosed inside the wall and she must have fallen asleep as when she came awake later, it felt like a lot of time had passed. When she checked on the dragon's room again, she could see there was no light but it was late enough that he might have gone to sleep already.

Taking a risk, Hermia crept out of her hiding place and entered the dragon's room.

Gideon opened up an eye when he heard the handle to his bedroom turn. He saw it open and a young girl slipped in. He hadn't thought that the Duke was the kind of man to send guests. He didn't particularly like a girl to entertain them. The girl didn't have a weapon so she wasn't sent to kill him either.

Gideon closed his eyes so he saw only through his eyelashes as the girl crouched by his bed and shook him awake. He opened his eyes but didn't move.

She whispered, "Are you really a dragon?"

Gideon nodded his head slightly. Curious about the girl. The girl let out a breath of relief. "You need to get me out of here. I thought the Duke was a good guy but he is really trying to take over the throne and he is going to use me. My aunt is the Empress."

Gideon asked, "Hermia?"

"You know who I am?" Her voice was a mixture of hope and surprise.

"The Emperor sent us here to get you out. Come." Gideon got out of the bed. Hermia stumbled back, surprised by his movement. Gideon had on pyjama pants. He had purchased them for when he slept in Hara's bed. She wasn't ready for him to be naked. But since they were in enemy territory, he had thought clothes in bed might be a good idea. He didn't add a shirt or even shoes as he went to the connecting door.

Hermia frowned and asked, "Who are you taking me to?"

Gideon pointed to one brand on his shoulder. "My mate is in the other room. She will know how to get you out of here without much trouble."

Hermia asked, "Your mate?"

He nodded. "She is the Captain of the Blazing Blunderbuss. She will sort things out."

Hermia looked worried and he glanced at her with his hand on the handle of the door. He frowned at her creased brow and asked, "What are you worried about?"

She cleared her throat a little. "She won't mind that there was a girl in your room while you are… well, almost naked?"

Gideon flashed a brief grin. "Oh, I really do hope she minds."

He didn't let her reply to that before he opened the door and went through. Hara was still awake. She was drawing some designs at the small writing desk. She was muttering to herself and put up a hand to indicate that they should wait. Gideon didn't mind. He also liked to be left alone whenever he was working. He rocked back and forth on his heels and put his hands in his pockets.

Hermia asked in a whisper, "Is she angry that you just barged in?"

Gideon almost laughed at the concept. "Unlikely. Annoyed? Maybe, but I barge in all the time. She is pretty when she argues so sometimes I do things to annoy her."

Hara said without looking up, "Your breathing annoys me."

She finished what she was working on and stood up. She looked at Hermia up and down and Gideon said, "This is the girl we came to retrieve."

Hara raised an eyebrow. "I gathered that. I know you like to collect things but you don't usually bring girls to my room. Unless you want her for our crew."

Gideon brightened at this suggestion and turned to study the noble woman a little closer. She dressed in a simple gown so she wasn't the kind that liked to dress up to the nines. She really wasn't suited for Demetrius, who still complained about the clothes Alice had rummaged up for him.

Gideon asked, "That is a good idea. We are shorthanded. Are you good at anything?"

Hermia stared at him as if he had grown another head by asking such a personal question.

Hara said, "Surely this could wait for later. We need to get out of here with the girl and the sooner the better."

Gideon shrugged. They could find out later what the girl was good at as he had a feeling she would be a good crew member.

Hara asked, "Have they been keeping you locked up?"

Hermia shook her head. "The Duke has been playing nice. He wants to seduce me as he doesn't have any clergy in his pocket yet. Though I bet soon he will turn to threats if I don't come around fast enough for him. But that does mean I get to move around freely. Though since you have arrived there have been a lot of soldiers around that weren't there before. They have been keeping a close watch on me. I had to sneak out."

"How long before they realise you are missing?"

"Not long." Hara looked at Gideon and he nodded. Now was better than later, as far as he was concerned.

He asked, "You want me to put on a distraction. Say twenty minutes?"

"Yes. West wall, thank you. See you on the ship."

He leaned forward and kissed her on Hara's cheek before he headed back toward his room. "See you on the ship, sweetheart."

Hara grumbled. "I hate it when you call me sweetheart."

He turned and backed out of the room with his hand on his chest, as if she had pierced him through his heart. Hara returned his smile briefly before she turned back to Hermia and Gideon could hear them setting out plans as he dressed.

Hara turned to her gear, which she had left on her bed when she had entered. She strapped it on. Hermia shifted from foot to foot nervously.

Eventually, Hermia asked, "As simple as that?"

Hara looked up from buckling on her tool belt. "Hardly. Let's go and wake the others and hope we don't run into any soldiers."

Thinking about the chances of running into soldiers, she palmed some of her net balls which could trap any soldiers they encountered and motioned to the girl to follow her. The others' rooms were across the hall. Hara knocked on the first door.

Murphy answered.

"We have the girl," Hara said simply. She motioned with her head over her shoulder. Murphy blinked and went onto his toes to look over Hara's shoulder. Hermia was hiding behind Hara.

Murphy gave the girl a grin. "What is the plan, Captain?"

"Grab the others and get the ship ready. Gideon is going to distract the men on the walls in about twenty minutes and I want everyone on board by then. Oh, and try to avoid killing anyone. The others aren't keen on it."

Murphy gave her a mock salute and wandered off in the direction of the other rooms.

Hermia asked, "Aren't we staying with them?"

Hara shook her head. "They will be the secondary distraction as Murphy can't sneak. Don't worry, they are good at making a noise. We will head along the wall to the ship. They will go through the courtyard."

Hara took her around a corner and they almost stumbled over a guard. Hara flicked the net ball and pulled Hermia back behind the corner of the wall. The soldier shot off a crossbow and then yelled.

Hara quickly looked around the corner. The man had dropped his crossbow when he had gone down. He was now swearing and trying to free himself from the fine net which had emerged from the small metal ball. Hara ran up to him and kicked him in his head. He went down then and didn't move.

Hara picked up his crossbow and nocked an arrow. Hermia stumbled behind her as she was watching the soldier.

Hara gave a concerned glance back at the girl, who muttered, "Why didn't I think of that?"

Hara raised an eyebrow at the comment that was obviously directed to herself. They didn't have time for a discussion though so Hara guided Hermia to the stairs which would lead them both up onto the walls.

Hara waited at the door at the top. There was a tremendous crash and then running feet and people yelling. Hara kicked open the door and shot at the startled soldier who had been about to open the door. He dived and stumbled over the edge of the wall, falling into the courtyard.

Hara looked over the wall he had fallen over. He had landed on a shed three storeys below. He groaned but didn't move. She doubted he would be trouble.

Hara took in the rest of the soldiers on the wall. They were all running towards Gideon, who was sitting on the west tower in all his dragon glory. He was sending flames above the heads of the soldiers and growling at them. Hara thought he might swipe at them like a cat next. It was clear he was only playing with them.

The Blazing Blunderbuss was moored to the tower on the other side of the castle. And there were only a few soldiers, and all their attention was on Gideon.

Hermia stumbled. "Is that the Dragon?"

Hara raised an eyebrow because it was obviously a dumb question. Gideon was in his full dragon-ness, his wings clamped to his back so he looked like a lizard that had been hit by a growth serum. His gold scales gleamed in the firelight of the watchtowers.

That strange feeling that wanted her to yell that he was hers made Hara grumble. Instead, Hara motioned for the girl, Hermia, to follow. They were almost below the airship when the soldiers realised they were there. Hara wasn't concerned. She had rolled a couple of net balls while they had still been watching Gideon and by the time they turned; the ball was shooting out a fine net over them.

The net was made from silk and surprisingly strong when made into a rope. A rope ladder dropped when they were finally under the ship.

Alice looked over the edge. "You better hurry." Alice waved towards Gideon to explain her concern.

Gideon was in the air now and Hara knew he was about to fly off. Hara swore when she saw two large automata climbing the walls of the castle. No wonder he was deciding to retreat.

Hara caught Hermia's shoulder and snapped urgently, "Climb!"

Hara looked up at Alice. "Are the others back?"

Alice shook her head. "Demetrius is missing."

Hara swore. But he was a nobleman and the Duke couldn't afford to have the boy killed quite yet, especially now that they had Hermia. Hara climbed up after Hermia. Angry that she had lost the boy.

Once on board, Hara said to Alice, "Take us away from the castle. We can't afford to be a target."

Alice hesitated. Alice hadn't gotten along with the young nobleman but it wasn't like Hara to leave someone behind.

Hermia said, "Demetrius is here? Why would he do that?"

Alice pursed her lips and left to follow Hara's orders while Hara answered Hermia. Hara knew that Alice would have a few choice words for her later, but Hara would take them as she deserved it. Hermia was the important one. Without her, the Duke's plans would have to be slowed. Maybe hindered enough that they could get Demetrius back intact.

Hara caught Hermia's arm and guided her further into the ship. "When Demetrius heard we were coming for you, he insisted on tagging along. He wanted you to get to know him before you returned to your family."

Hermia frowned. "I don't want to go home."

"Well, that is good because we aren't going anywhere until we rescue Demetrius. And we have a passenger to drop off."

Liam skidded into the hallway. "Murphy has been hurt."

Hara swore softly to herself. "How bad?"

"He'll live. But he needs some stitches. I know you taught me how to do them but he wriggles a lot. I mean, like a lot."

Hara would have done it herself but she had to give more instructions to Alice. They couldn't just leave without Demetrius and they couldn't stick around either.

Hermia said, "I have a fine hand at needlework. If you can get him to be still, I'll do the sewing."

Liam looked at Hara to see if it was all right to make a noblewoman stitch up someone. Hara nodded. If anyone could make fine stitches, it would be a noble woman and said to Liam, "Give him something to bite on. That way, he is less likely to swear like a bloody sailor."

Liam's concern disappeared under the brief grin he gave Hara.

"Come this way, my ladyship. Murphy is mostly harmless," he said reassuringly.

Hara went onto the bridge. The sky was clear, so the automata were ground only. But they hadn't heard that Duke had automata from the Emperor or Harlen so the Duke clearly had secrets and might have other things hidden away.

The whole ship dipped, signalling that Gideon must have landed. He must be in a bad way if he was not changing just as he came to the ship as he liked to make a game of it.

Hara said, "Put us behind that mountain there. They won't be able to see us from the castle but we will remain close enough to get Demetrius back."

Alice looked relieved as she followed Hara's orders. Alice said, "I know he is a nuisance but you aren't one to leave anyone behind."

Gideon came in, playing with the torn edges of his shirt. "I liked this shirt, you know. I really should shift naked. It will have less of an impact on my clothing."

He looked up at Hara and then quickly made up the distance between them. He frowned at Hara and she realised she must not have concealed her concern for Demetrius very well.

It was easier to allow her emotions out and stepped into Gideon's embrace. He tightened his arms around her but he had hesitated. Probably surprised that she had accepted his comfort.

Hara mumbled, "I lost Demetrius."

"Dead lost or just lost like a puppy lost?" he asked softly.

Hara couldn't help but smile against Gideon's chest. "Puppy lost."

"Ah," Gideon said sagely. He pressed his nose to her hair. "You are just like a dragon. We will get him back."

Liam came running onto the bridge. He had his hands clasped around something. Hara pulled away from Gideon to see what Liam had brought them. When Liam opened his hands, he had a small clockwork creature.

It looked like a hummingbird and was about the same size. In its beak was a rolled up note. Liam kept the clockwork bird trapped in his hands as Hara pulled out the wedged note. She unrolled it and frowned at the words.

Gideon asked, "What does it say? Who is the bird from?"

"The Duke says he has Demetrius and unless we give back Hermia, he will kill the boy."

Liam added, "Also, there was an airship and it left from the castle. It is heading out of the Empire."

"We are heading that way next to drop off our passenger. Do you think Demetrius is on that airship?"

Gideon asked, "Do you want me to go find out?"

"No, they will be expecting a dragon. They might have something to combat you." And she had already lost one person she didn't want to lose another.

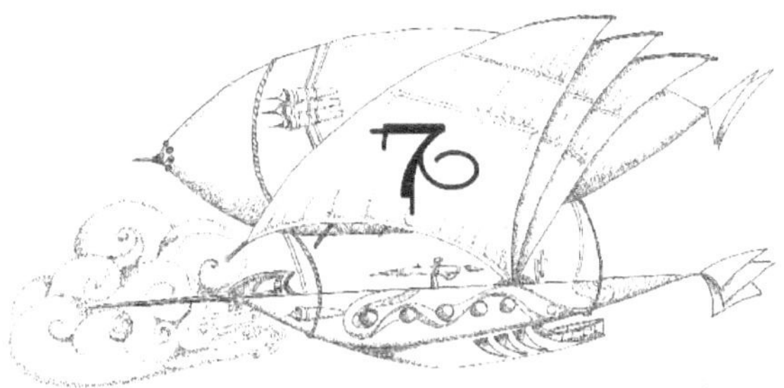

T he girl from dinner knocked on Demetrius's door. He frowned at her, wondering why Helena would bother with him. She had hardly paid any attention to him throughout dinner. Now she was batting flirtatious eyes at him and had her assets thrust out for his perusal.

She reached out and ran a hand over his arm. "Demetrius, I am so glad you answered the door. I wanted to get to know you better."

His frown deepened. "You didn't seem to want to do that earlier."

She waved his concerns off with a flick of her hand. "Not when the Duke is around. He is a very jealous man and I wouldn't want you to be hurt if he thought my attention was attracted by your fine frame."

Demetrius blushed at her words. He cleared his throat. "I'm betrothed."

Helena snorted with derision. "And she doesn't want you as much as I want you. Come with me and we'll go somewhere private where I can show you just how much I want you."

Demetrius hesitated. He was here to rescue Hermia. He wasn't here for his own amusement, but they hadn't even seen Hermia yet. She might not have reached the

Duke's castle yet or might have already left. There was no guarantee that they would ever find her and Helena sure was pretty.

Helena didn't wait for him to make up his mind and slid her hand down his arm to his and tugged on it, leading him out of the room. They didn't go far as Helena opened a door and led him into a dimly lit room just down the hall.

He asked, "Do you want me to light a candle?"

Helena purred. "I like the dark. Come over here."

She guided him through the dark room and turned him around and pushed him back. He floundered for a moment before he fell back onto a chair. Helena let him go but he stayed in the chair trying to make out her shape in the dark. Something landed around his arms. "What was that?"

Helena pressed her lips against his ear and whispered, "Trust me, you will like this. I know how to make it good for you."

Demetrius had moved his hand to figure out what was around him. It felt like a rope. He had heard of women who tied up their men but he had never been involved in anything like that. He hesitated, wondering if he should mention that he wasn't into ropes and tying when the slack in the rope went tight.

He oomphed as Helena had pulled tight enough that he was forced to breathe out. He tried to push the rope up and over his head but another length of rope fell over his arms.

He said timidly, "I don't think I like this."

The ropes over his arms went tight before he could tug them free. His panic rose.

He asked, worried, "Helena? Can we stop now?"

He was struggling in earnest now as he really didn't want to be in this situation. He jerked when Helena sat in his lap. She looped the rope around him a few more times, then leaned against him to tie it at the back.

Demetrius knew he shouldn't be distracted by the voluptuous flesh that was pressed against him but it took him a few moments to remember he was trying to escape and to continue his struggles. The struggle and the fact that Helena was on his lap made things uncomfortable for him. But she soon left his lap and he couldn't even hear her moving around the room.

He asked of the darkness, "Helena?"

But there was only silence. He tried again to loosen the ropes so he could escape but the little minx had a good hand at knots. Sometime later, the door opened and a large figure entered.

The Duke said, "You could have lit a light, my dear."

Demetrius' blood went cold. If the Duke found him in Helena's room, he might think they were up to something and Demetrius knew the Duke would not appreciate that he had designs on his mistress. Demetrius kept still, hoping when the Duke realised Helena wasn't in the room that he would just leave.

But Helena said from the shadows, "A light reveals everything, my love."

A flash of light and the Duke lit a gas lantern attached to the wall by the door. The light revealed that they weren't even in a bedroom. The only piece of furniture was the chair Demetrius was tied to. There weren't even windows in the room.

Dread filled Demetrius. Things obviously weren't as they seemed. The Duke turned to Demetrius. "Well, isn't this a surprise? You are going to be our guest while we question you."

Demetrius firmed his jaw and said as bravely as he could, "You won't get anything from me."

He jerked when a blade was laid against his cheek. The cold spread from the blade as Helena said softly by his ear, "You will tell us everything or you will lose body parts you had intended to put to use tonight."

Demetrius swallowed a lump in his throat. Hara was going to kill him for messing up their plans.

⸺⸺⸺⸺⸺

Demetrius hung against the ropes that held him to the chair. Everything stung with fresh pain as the Duke doused his wounds with alcohol. Demetrius tensed and gritted his teeth. The world seemed to melt around him and even words seemed half melted but he managed to make out, "Useless — Waste of time — he is your — fine."

The next thing Demetrius was aware of was someone pressing a flask to his lips. He gulped down the water. The world around him came into sharp focus, and he could feel every injury upon his body. He swallowed the water and opened his eyes to see Helena making sure his thirst was quenched.

Helena had an odd look on her face which he couldn't decipher. She cradled his head and offered him some more. Quenched, he leaned back so he wasn't pressed up against the ropes.

Demetrius asked, "So, what is in it for you? Are you planning to be his whore while Hermia is his Empress?"

Helena didn't answer. She turned and rummaged in a bag and brought out some food for him. With his hands tied, he was forced to let her feed him. He wanted to spit it on her. But he was weak from the torture and needed all the sustenance he could get.

The Captain would come for him soon and he would need his strength if he was going to escape.

When Helena spoke, it took him a while to realise that she was answering his question from before. "Nothing really. I grew up poor. You wouldn't know what that means but when I was four, some men came to our village. They took me and my siblings. They raised us for their use and when I was old enough, they sent us into the world to do their bidding. I am here not because I think the Duke can give me anything, instead I am here for my country."

Her accent gave away her country of origin. "Rosh?"

"We are Rosh now. We weren't always Rosh. But my people had a choice: be taken over by the Empire or turn to Rosh."

"The Empire isn't that bad." There was a look of longing in Helena's eyes but she hid it quickly so that Demetrius wasn't even sure he had seen it. The door opened with some force and Duke Lysander entered the room, along with several soldiers.

The Duke said to Helena, "Is he able to travel?"

Helena looked Demetrius over. "He will live."

The Duke flicked his hand to order the soldiers to take him. Demetrius waited for them to release his bonds and then he would make his move. Unfortunately, the only move he made was to fall forward onto his face.

He struggled to bring up his arms to stop his fall but he had been in one position for too long and his limbs didn't respond to him the way he wanted them to. Helena caught him at the last moment but before he could take advantage of her being close and maybe taking her as a hostage, two of the soldiers pulled him to his feet.

They tied his arms behind him with enough force that Demetrius grunted with pain. Several of the cuts on his arms and chest bled again. His shirt was little more than rags but he wished they had removed it as he didn't want to wait for the fibres to dry and stick to his wounds.

Demetrius tried to struggle against the soldiers but they merely picked him up by his elbows and dragged him outside after the Duke.

Helena asked, "What was the commotion before?"

Demetrius frowned. He hadn't heard anything before which meant he had been unconscious through whatever commotion Helena was talking about.

The Duke growled. "They got the girl. I don't know how they found her but they left with her. The boy is the bait now so he will live until we can get the girl back. You are to make sure he doesn't die."

"And the weapons," she asked cryptically so he wouldn't know everything they planned.

"The Engineer is still busy but he informed me the first batch is ready and waiting to be picked up. That is where we are going. We will take the boy and see if we can lure the dragon and his whore of a mate out into the open. Once there, we can take them and the girl back and our plans will be back on schedule." The Duke answered her as if she were a servant rather than a partner with brusqueness rather than sweetness.

The door opened and the light made Demetrius squint. He hadn't realised it was dawn already. The soldiers dragged him to an airship. One that Demetrius hadn't seen moored at the castle before, so it must have only arrived shortly before. It was larger than the Blazing Blunderbuss and it bristled with weapons.

There was no way that the Blazing Blunderbuss could take on the Duke's airship, even with Gideon as a dragon. Demetrius' heart dropped. He wasn't going to be saved any time soon. Demetrius looked around for the Blazing Blunderbuss, though he knew he wouldn't see it.

His heart wanted it to be close, to swoop out of the sky and rescue him but it seemed that it would be up to him to have to rescue himself.

The soldiers dumped him in a small room that had no furniture but a single chair. Helena entered behind him and made sure that his hands were secured to the chair.

Helena patted his cheek. "You are lucky. The Duke planned to kill you once you had given him all the information he was looking for. When you proved to know nothing, he was going to throw you from the parapets as a warning to your smuggler friends they shouldn't mess with him. You get to live another day."

She then sauntered out of the room and Demetrius wanted to leap up and strangle her. How could she work for a foul man like the Duke? What was it about the men that made women think they were going to be their saviour? If the Duke hadn't been so charming, Hermia would never have walked into his home and they wouldn't have been in this situation at all.

Defeated, Demetrius hung his head and thought miserably. At least now he had his adventure.

<hr>

The mood around the mess table was sombre. Murphy asked, "We going back for the boy?"

Alice interrupted any answer Hara could have given by saying, "He was stupid enough to get caught."

Liam said, "But we still need to rescue him."

Hermia said in a soft voice, "It is all my fault."

Hara said, "It isn't your fault. I should have kept him by my side. I knew he would get into trouble. But we will rescue him."

There was a long silence, then Murphy braved the silence. "So, what is the plan? Storm the castle and raze it to the ground?"

Talen said, "That is stupid. We are a small group and they almost had us and all we were doing was escaping."

Liam added helpfully, "And rescuing a princess."

Hermia blushed. "I'm not a princess."

Liam smiled at her and Murphy slapped Liam on his back and cheered him on. "Go on, you mate. She is on the rebound so she should be easy."

Alice made a sound of disgust and leaned over to Hermia. "Ignore them. Their brains are south of their belts when it comes to women."

Gideon brought the conversation back to normalcy. "I can't attack the castle while the automata are there."

Liam cleared his throat and everyone turned to him. He flushed, then said, "I might — I think I can help with that. But I'll need a few days to make something to use. I don't know if it will work."

Hara nodded at her apprentice. "Work on that. We have other leads to follow. First, we follow that airship. We will drop off our passenger and catch up with the airship and get Demetrius."

Alice asked, "Are you sure he is on the airship?"

If Demetrius was left behind, he might be safer but she doubted they would lose the opportunity to get to know them better by interrogating Demetrius. "Most likely. They won't leave him at the castle. The Duke likes to control things too much to leave something like a prisoner in the hands of someone else." Hopefully they weren't too vigorous in their questioning.

Hermia agreed. "Yes, the Duke is a control freak. Always has been. He'll have Demetrius with him."

No one mentioned that there was a chance that the Duke wasn't on the airship either. But it was the only thing they could do immediately.

Hara said to Alice, "Set a course to follow that airship."

Alice got to her feet. "A good idea to get rid of the passenger. It isn't like we can start a small war with him on board in any case."

Murphy grinned. "Speak for yourself."

With Alice's departure, it was a signal to the others that the meeting was over. Liam said, "I better get to work."

He disappeared quickly. Hara would find him later to see if she could help him with whatever plan he had to deal with the automata Hermia stayed though and stared at her hands.

Hara asked, "What is it, Hermia?"

The young woman looked up. "I don't want anyone to get hurt because of me."

Hara looked at Hermia with sympathy. "No one will be hurt because of you, Hermia. They will be hurt because a man thought he could rise to be an emperor without first paying his dues. He wanted to use you as a shortcut but that isn't his right. In fact, you have helped. I'm sure Murphy is happy you have a dab hand at stitches."

Gideon added his own two cents. "Young people like you make mistakes. It is part of becoming a human being. Learn from it and move on."

Hara glanced at Gideon, surprised by the sound advice. "I agree. Don't dwell on it."

Hermia got to her feet. Her hands holding each other tight enough that her knuckles were white. "I'll try."

Hermia hustled off. Hara turned to Gideon, who was leaning against the wall. He had Angel curled around his neck and was handing her nuts to hold in her small claws.

Gideon looked at her as he said, "Are you going to blame yourself for the boy?"

Hara said, "Most likely."

Gideon asked in a purr, "Want me to help you forget for a while?"

She was tempted to invite him to her room but she knew it would only be a reaction instead of a decision so she shook her head. Gideon looked at her with hot eyes but didn't pressure her.

Hara gave him something. "I do think I love you, you know."

His smile grew slowly from one side of his mouth to the other before he said, "I know."

***

It was quiet on the bridge when Hermia walked in cautiously.

Hara let her settle before she said anything. "Worried?" It wasn't really a question as it was late and Hermia had been up all the night before.

For her to be here now meant she hadn't been able to sleep at all. Dark shadows ringed her eyes.

Hermia fiddled with the hem on her shirt before she answered. "It is all my fault. I mean him being taken and all that."

"I thought we had clarified that the whole mess is the Duke's fault."

Hermia shook her head. "The Duke really wants me. I thought if we could talk to him and somehow get him to trade Demetrius for me, then everything will be alright."

Hara wanted to sigh but was afraid that she would offend the girl while she was in her tired state. "Everything wouldn't be alright. We would still have to rescue you. The Emperor won't pardon us of piracy if all we do is swap you for Demetrius."

Hermia turned angry and the emotion surprised Hara. She had thought the girl a bit of a mouse until now.

Hermia dashed to her feet and moved her arms violently to express herself. "You would let him die! Just for your pardon. What kind of people are you to condemn a man like that? He might be an arrogant lord but he didn't ask to be drawn into this mess. If I hadn't fallen into this trap, he would be fine. He wouldn't be a prisoner and probably being tortured and hurt."

Hara let her rant for a while and then said in a calm voice, "We aren't leaving Demetrius. But we aren't leaving you in the Duke's power either. You are tired and you are worried. It is understandable that you will be upset but things will seem calmer in the morning. Trust me."

Hermia gritted out. "How do you know? You have never been in this situation before. You don't know what it is like."

Hara leant on the helm, so she was a little closer to Hermia as she said, "When I was seventeen, my father was using me for his cons. We had these fake mines that we were convincing people to invest in. I was making these digging machines to show off to the clients. One day, during one of these demonstrations, one of the client's friends burst in with soldiers. He had been to the place my father insisted had a mine and had discovered there was nothing there. He had returned to arrest me and my father. My father set my machine to blow. I knew if it did, it would take out most of the building. So I stayed to stop it from blowing up." Hermia's eyes widened with surprise as Hara told her story.

"My father escaped and I stopped the main explosion, but I messed up and something blew anyway on the machine. It knocked me out. I woke up the next day in a dungeon. They didn't know that I was a girl, so they threw me into the general population. I got into quite a few fights that first day. But when the guards came to check on us, I told them I was a girl. It was a risk as I was still guilty of the crime I was in there for. I was lucky, though and the warden was curious. He had me brought to his house. He had heard of my grandfather, you see and knew that I had inherited his skills. He made a deal with me. If I worked in his house to modernise it, he would keep me out of the general population. I slept in his house. He was a better man than I knew as he spoke to the judge who was trying my case and convinced him I was better off working for my crime than spending it in a jail. So when my case was heard, I was sentenced to create engines for the navy for three years."

Hara's voice grew fierce as she continued, "So don't tell me I don't know. I know what it means to not know what is going to happen and the nicest thing is still a terrible future. I know what it feels like to blame yourself when it really isn't your fault. It took me years to even get over what my father did to me and even talk to him. Okay, he isn't in my life now but that is his choice, not mine. I have moved on and I'm better for it. So let time pass and stay calm. Things will come right if you focus on what you can do rather than all that went wrong."

Hermia was pale as she rolled on her heels and mashed up the hem of her shirt in her fists.

Eventually she said, "I'm nobody. I might be related to the Empress but really I'm nobody. I have four brothers. No one cares what happens to me. The only reason I got any education was because they told the tutors to teach all the children because they were too cheap to get me my own tutors. And the tutors only knew how to teach boys so they taught me what they were teaching the others. I don't know what to do with all this—attention." She struggled to find the right word.

Hara gave her an enigmatic smile. "We never know what to do with all this attention."

Hara meant Gideon. She hadn't known what to do about his attraction to her and was still afraid of what it all meant.

Hara said to Talen as their passenger Puck left the Blazing Blunderbuss. "Follow him."

Talen nodded and disappeared. Alice, who was standing with Hara on the deck, asked, "Do you think he has secrets?"

"Yes. It was too convenient that the Duke knew who Demetrius was. We had come straight from court. So it couldn't be rumours and it couldn't have been a spy at court because our ship is faster than almost anything but a royal courier ship. He must have been the one to talk to the Duke."

Alice frowned. "Are you sure the Duke didn't figure out who he was because the Duke and Demetrius are both nobles?"

Hara leant on the railing to look at the figure of Talen disappearing in the crowd after Puck. "No. Demetrius might be betrothed to the Empress' niece but he really is a nobody in the noble world. His parents own a harbour port and they are pretty much chained to their business. They never come to court. The Duke on the other hand is a local to the mountains. He seduced the only daughter of a lord and married her. A year after her father died and passed on his title to Lysander, she also disappeared. Duke Lysander has been keeping low. Neither

Demetrius nor Duke Lysander would have been in the same circles. He wouldn't have known Demetrius, from a look. Someone had to tell the Duke that Demetrius was Hermia's groom. Even Hermia wouldn't have been able to point out her groom."

Hara was sure Puck had a part to play in this drama. And those machine parts in that room in the castle's basement made her think he might be the brawn behind the Duke. It was a risk to let the engineer return to his master but hopefully it would lead them to Demetrius.

Alice said, "There is a ship in port that is very similar to the one we saw leaving the Duke's castle."

Hara looked at Alice with surprise. Hara hadn't realised the girl was so adapt at recognising ships to be able to tell them apart. After all, the ship they had seen leaving the Duke's castle had been in the distance and in the semi-dark of dawn.

There were several ships in the large trader port and they were obscured by each other. Before Hara could ask for more details, Liam was calling for her. They had worked through the night on the project to deal with the large automata. Liam had really come into his own in the last year.

He was a worthy apprentice for her Opa's knowledge.

***

Talen returned in the early afternoon. He took Hara aside to tell her what he found. He glared at Gideon, who moved from his place at the bridge window to be close enough to hear what Talen reported.

Hara said to Talen when she saw the look, "I trust him, Talen."

Talen narrowed his eyes as he studied her. "You have never trusted anyone before."

"And there is a reason for that. You know better than anyone what I had to go through with my father." Talen had a skewed view of her father and to him, her father could do no wrong.

Gideon growled at the mention of her father and said in a rough voice, "He will not bother you anymore."

Talen dropped it. "I followed that strange man and he went to an airship with the Duke's emblem on it. They were loading up gear so I don't think they will be in port for very long. What do you want me to do now? Sneak on board to see if the boy is there?"

"No. We need to deal with whatever the Duke is planning in any case. We can't leave him as a threat and just rescue Demetrius. We will take a few of us to see if we can delay them. Hopefully, by then we can come up with a plan to not only stop the Duke but to rescue Demetrius without him being hurt."

"Don't you think leaving him in the Duke's clutches will put him in danger?" Talen asked with a frown on his brow.

"No, as Demetrius is bait for Hermia. If Demetrius fell into the trap to get Hermia, she will feel obligated to rescue him. The Duke is hoping because Hermia is a girl she will simply trade herself." Hara was worried about Demetrius but she didn't think his life was in danger. At least not yet. Duke Lysander had already proved he could kill someone when he had his wife killed. Demetrius was still in a lot of danger.

Hara had already spoken to Hermia about the foolhardiness of trading herself to the Duke. It wouldn't solve anything and only put them in the same trouble as before.

It was harder getting past the guards at the port than expected. They had left Murphy and Liam the task of distracting the guards while the rest of them snuck into the area reserved for the Duke's airship. Alice and Henry had remained with the Blazing Blunderbuss so that meant Hara was left with Gideon and Talen and the two men bickered the whole time.

Hara hissed at them as they crouched behind a crate. "If the two of you don't stop arguing, I'm going to make you walk back to the ship by yourself." The two stared glumly at each other with pursed lips. Hara sighed. "I should have taken Murphy and Liam."

Now that the two were quiet, she took the risk of scouting out the area more. The Duke wasn't in sight and neither was Puck. Helena, though, was directing men to load several large crates onto the airship. They seemed heavy and that made Hara curious. Obviously, they were here to pick up something and not just the engineer, Puck.

If the Duke was involved, Hara would bet it had something to do with weapons. As you didn't take on an Empire run by dragons without first stocking up on the biggest cannons you could find.

Hara said without looking at Talen or Gideon, "Talen, you get onto the ship and see if you can find Demetrius. Gideon and I are going to see what is in those crates and maybe make a distraction by having a little chat with Helena. Who seems much further into this than a mere mistress would normally be?"

Talen slinked off without a word. Hara glanced back to see if Gideon was alright with the plan. He was watching Helena, who was signing something off from the man who had delivered the crates. If they couldn't get into the crates, that form would probably give them an idea of what was in the crates. So they would go after the girl first.

Hara waited for a moment when there was some commotion while the porters handled the crates and moved forward. Gideon was silent as he followed behind her. Hara wasn't worried that he would be left behind as he always seemed to be there.

Hara pulled out a gun and made sure it was loaded and waited for a moment when Helena's attention was elsewhere. But before that moment arrived, there was a yell and someone pointed to Talen. Talen turned to run but went smack into a guard and landed on his back. He scrambled to his feet and ran for it. The place was like a beehive knocked over and porters and guards were chasing after Talen. So much for him going after Demetrius.

One soldier approached Helena and they spoke softly so Hara couldn't make out what they were saying. Helena then took the lift up to the airship and left the soldiers to finish the loading of the crates. The soldiers seemed more concerned about chasing down Talen than searching for others around the perimeter of the loading area.

Gideon moved first out of cover to the closest crate. It was set on a trolley to be moved onto the lift. Hara muttered a few choice swear words to herself before she followed him. Once there, they were still undercover. There was a loud bang and smoke filled the air in the distance.

Several soldiers ran off to see what the new commotion was about. Gideon pushed the crate until it was on the lift. Hara turned the handle and the crate and lift rose to the airship above.

Hara realised Gideon wasn't hiding as they were rising and caught his arm and dragged him down so they would both be hidden by the crate to any casual view.

She hissed at Gideon. "Behave or we will be in trouble and we already have been taken prisoner a few times. I don't want to repeat that pattern again."

But when they reached the top, there was no one there. They pushed the crate into the hold and moved to hide. Hopefully, if anyone discovered the crate was already in the hold, they would assume that the porters had loaded it.

The hold was filled with the crates and with strange large jars. Hara went to investigate the crates while Gideon looked over the jars. Inside one crate was a small humming bird made of clockwork. It was the same design as the one that had delivered the Duke's message but these were also mostly vials.

She twisted one around and saw that there were two syringes attached to its body. It was designed to land on someone or something and inject it like a bee would. The syringes were empty and that made Hara look towards the jars.

She asked, "What are in them?"

Gideon had the lid off the first one and sniffed. "Almonds. Mm, cyanide?"

"Poison." Hara looked back at the crates and swore. "They have those blasted bird things with syringes. They are going to get them to inject people. Is it cyanide in the other jar?"

He opened the jar and stumbled backwards. Hara looked at him with concern. "What?"

"It is the poison the crazy scientist who wanted to defect to Rosh made." His voice was grave with anger.

Hara swore. "How the hell did the Duke get hold of that. I thought we had destroyed it and the scientist is being held by the Empire?"

"But he is still working for the Empire." Gideon's voice was incredulous.

"Damn, that is why Puck was in Versailles. He was finding out the recipe. He must have sent it ahead with one of his bloody birds."

Last year, they had come across a scientist who had accidentally discovered a poison that only killed dragons. Rosh had planned to release it somehow and kill a lot of dragons. If Puck knew how to kill dragons, then there would be no stopping the Duke and his army.

When the automata arrived on the battlefield, the Emperor would send his heavy guns, the dragons. Only with the birds that would kill both soldiers and dragon alike.

Gideon reached out a cautious hand to the poison jars and they popped out of existence. Dragons had the ability to move things into another place. It was how they changed their shape. With them gone Hara breathed a sigh of relief but that didn't stop the Duke or Puck who had the recipe for the poison. There was no way they could leave the Duke and Puck as they were to continue on with their plans.

Hara motioned to the crates of mechanical humming birds. "Can you make those disappear as well?"

She passed him the bird she had in her hand. He took it and frowned and looked up. "I can't."

He turned the bird around and swore.

Hara asked, "What is it?"

"It is made with ebony and ivory."

Hara wasn't sure why that was so important, though that made these probably very expensive little mechanical birds.

Gideon scraped with a fingernail at one eye. "And quartz. This isn't good. There are very few people that know all three of the elements."

Hara asked, "What does it mean?"

"We have a traitor. You see, when we came over from our world. Dragons, I mean, when we came over, we were shooting into the dark. We wanted a world that could be pleasant and liveable. We needed some elements that were the same between both our world and this one. But our world had come close to a comet and the surface was fried. There were no trees or plants left for us to use. And even if there were, we didn't want elements that were too common on this world as it would make us vulnerable. So we picked ebony. As it was once alive. Ivory as it is, both alive and dead. And last quartz as it can grow but is dead at the same time. This dual nature made it very suitable for our needs. But whenever we are held in the grasp of one of those elements of our ability to move to the other place, to the place of nowhere is hindered." Gideon paced nervously. She would never associate with him nervousness so she was also worried.

"If we are attacked with these birds, we will have no way to stop them. To crush them will release the poison. Whoever made up this plan has to be a dragon."

Hara gaped. "Who? I mean, who would let a madman loose with the way to kill dragons?"

"Only bonded dragons. It doesn't hurt those that aren't bonded. It could be a dragon who is not bonded."

Hara stared at Gideon as the realisation sunk into her with cold horror. It made such logical sense and yet it made her sick to even think about it. The Emperor and his family encouraged dragons to mate with humans. They were the bonded ones. Only the dragons who weren't bonded were at odds with the Empire. She had even met a few.

She asked, "Do you think it is someone close to the Emperor? Your brother?"

Gideon's look darkened. "It would have to be someone at court and who is trusted, as I doubt they would have trusted the secret of the poison to just any dragon."

"They might have if they thought it would be crazy to release a poison like this on the world."

"There are crazy dragons." Gideon stated coldly.

"There has to be but Gideon, we can't let them get away with this. This is too dangerous. If we leave them to their own devices, they might come after you. You are the Emperor's great uncle. They will see you as part of the whole thing they are trying to get rid of and I am sick and tired of looking over my shoulder. We have to take them down, even if it means we have to step up from mayhem to some bloodshed."

Gideon gave her a dark look. "I have never eaten a human but I have killed before." Enough said.

The airship shuddered and moved. Any plans to stop the airship while it was still in port were out of the question. They couldn't just make the crates disappear as Gideon had done to the poisons so they would have to dispose of the cargo before someone came down here to check on it.

The airship had left in a hurry so the crew would probably wait until they were over the sea before they came down here to check on the cargo. That gave them a little time.

Hara went over to the edge of the deck and looked down. They were still over land but already Hara could see the sea. The water wouldn't have to be very deep, as the salt water alone would corrode the delicate parts of the humming bird mechanicals. There were several crates and they were heavy.

Hara turned to Gideon and hissed. "Hurry, we need to move them over here."

It would make the airship flounder if they shifted the cargo and it would send the crew down earlier so they would have to work fast. It was awkward work to load the crates on the small dolly and man handle them towards the edge of the deck.

They turned when they heard some footsteps. Hara left Gideon and rushed to the door. Hara threw a few net balls down the corridor and ran back to Gideon. He had the last crate near the edge. Hara looked over the edge of the deck. There was water beneath them and the yelling from the corridor meant they were running out of time. Without any words needed between the two of them, they shoved the crates over the edge.

The wooden boxes whistled as they flew and thankfully the lids stayed on the crates and none of the mechanical birds flew free. They could hear the distant splash as the boxes landed in the ocean.

Once that was done Hara looked around for a place they could hide once the crew figured out how to get free of the nets and came after them. But they had just thrown all their covers into the ocean below. The first crew member got through and he pointed a gun at the two of them. Hara put her hands up and Gideon followed her.

Demetrius dozed. He had tried to sleep but the awkward angle he was tied in the chair meant that every time he fell asleep, his head fell forward and woke him. He didn't move, though, when he heard the door open.

Helena came in. She didn't have any food so she wasn't here to feed him. Instead, without even giving him a greeting, she went to pick up a bed pan.

Panic shot through Demetrius as he cleared his throat and asked hopefully, "Where is the other guy?"

He didn't suggest that he didn't need to relieve himself as he had been holding on for a while now.

Helena raised a curious eyebrow before she asked, "Never had a woman handle your junk before?"

Demetrius blushed and hated that his skin betrayed him. She stood with her free hand on her hip and looked him over appreciatively. "You aren't bad looking and you are a nobleman so it is a bit of a surprise that you haven't lured some servant girl into a darkened closet."

Demetrius snapped. "That isn't fair."

"No? Other men have done as such." Helena seemed astonished by his admission.

"Well, they lack honour. To take advantage of a girl whose livelihood depends on your family is dishonourable," Demetrius stated firmly.

"So no servant girls. You have money. Why haven't you paid for your pleasure then."

"That is just as deplorable. I have studied economics. I understand the laws of demand and supply. If men did not demand the women to service them, then those women would be somewhere else doing as they wished." Demetrius deplored noblemen who used their power against others even if they paid for the pleasure.

"Ah, well, I hadn't thought of it in a matter of economics." Helena wriggled the bedpan in her hand. "If you can hold it for longer, then you can probably wait for a crewman to free up."

"What happened to the other guy? The one that helped me before," he asked with only a little hope in his voice. If the man was going to be there, he would have arrived already. Helena was his only choice.

"We had to leave port quickly and we left some of our men on the ground. They will catch up with us later but that means we are a little shorthanded."

Demetrius thought about this for a while and knew he couldn't get Helena to help him with his business as it would start a whole host of other problems.

He asked, "Surely you can untie me. I swear I won't escape."

"You can't swear that. You have just said you are a man of honour and a man of honour will always try to escape from his captors even if that means lying. As to remain in our hands is to be used for nefarious purposes, which is dishonourable." When he gave her a surprised look, she snapped. "I read as well."

She waved the bedpan to indicate that he was to decide. He really couldn't wait much longer and he didn't relish the thought of sitting in his own mess.

He countered, "One hand."

Helena looked him over again with that appraising look, then nodded her head. She put the bed pan aside and then fidgeted with his ropes. His left hand became free. Eventually, she stepped back and placed the bedpan where it would be useful.

He moved his free hand and realised she had tied him up so his hand was free, but his shoulder and upper arm were still pinned to his side and the chair.

He said facetiously, "You are very good with ropes."

Helena flashed him a bright grin. "Many men have told me that."

"You have had the occasion to tie up a lot of men, I take it. I didn't realise that the Duke required so many prisoners."

Her eyes grew hot as she purred. "It was all for pleasure."

Demetrius blushed again when he realised she wasn't talking about tying up prisoners.

He asked instead to hide his embarrassment, "Aren't you going to give me some privacy?"

"No. You are young but you are also clever. I would be a fool to allow you to escape." She leaned against a wall so she could watch him carefully.

He sighed and she had probably seen everything he was about to show, anyway. He relieved himself self-consciously. He tucked himself away and Helena tied him up securely again. He had hoped she would forget and he would have a chance to escape. She was right. No matter what he promised, he would try to escape.

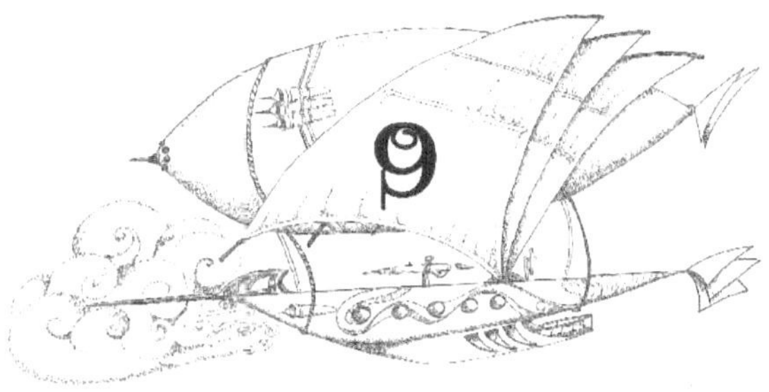

The Duke stepped past his men to glare at the two of them. He motioned to one of his men and Hara was thinking, this is it. He is going to have us shot and thrown off the edge of the deck. Instead, two men lugged out a steel mesh net. Before she could even get her mind around the contraption, the men were throwing the whole thing over the two of them.

The net was heavy and she oomphed as the air in her lungs was pushed out with the force of the net.

Gideon grumbled. "That boy better be worth this. The net is a dragon hunter net."

The Duke came to stand over the two of them to gloat. "Yes, when I knew I was going after the Empire, I knew I would have to neutralise the dragons as much as the Emperor's armies. It took a while to find a true dragon hunter. There aren't many around."

Gideon said, "There is a reason for that."

The Duke ignored Gideon's comment and motioned to his men again. This time, the two of them were bodily picked up. They were carried through the airship. The airship was bigger than the Blazing Blunderbuss but the corridors were still very narrow and Hara swore and cursed in pain every time the men knocked her into the walls.

They threw the two of them, still tied up in the net, into a room. "Damnit, Gideon, why does your butt have to be so bony?"

Gideon retorted, "For the same reason your elbow is. You are aware it is lodged very close to some very important parts of my body."

The door slammed. It was clear by the quiet afterwards that they had been left in the room without any guards. Hopefully she could figure a way out of the net but she was doubtful. The net, after all, was made to hold a dragon.

"Shush and help me roll over. We have to see where we are." Hara commanded before she tried to roll one way and he tried to roll the other.

Hara was almost elbowed in the temple and grumbled. "Left. Roll left."

The two of them rolled, this time in the same direction, and Gideon, with his head squished to the floor, said in a distorted voice, "I hope you didn't want kids. I think I got my manhood caught in the net."

His voice rising at the end of the sentence as she moved so she could get a better vantage of the room. Hara ignored him and looked around. It was almost completely empty of furniture except for a chair.

Hara smiled. "Hello, Demetrius."

The young man looked worse for wear and his face was a pretty rainbow of bruises but at least he was alive and relatively well.

Gideon asked, "He is alive?"

Hara answered, "Mostly."

"What do you mean by, mostly? Roll over so I can have a look." He wriggled under her but the net made it really difficult to move.

Demetrius said, "I'm alright. I can't believe the two of you came for me." His voice trembling with his relief and hope.

"Well, we were hoping to sneak in." Hara admitted and Gideon continued, "Best laid plans of mice and men, I'm afraid."

Hara shushed him. She wanted to ask Demetrius what he knew and Gideon could grumble for a while. Especially since she was lying on top of Gideon and he hated to feel trapped. He had a tendency to either act foppish or to grumble whenever he was trapped. "Do a maths equation Gideon I need to interrogate the young Lord so we can figure out a way to get out of here." Her only answer from Gideon was silence.

Hara turned her head a little so she could really take in Demetrius. They had used a copious amount of rope to tie him to the chair. She would ask about that later. His shirt was in tatters and his chest and arms were covered in scabbed over cuts. None of them looked infected but even though they weren't liable to kill him, he had obviously been through a lot of pain. Hara didn't want to dwell on the torture and instead asked, "How did they catch you?"

Demetrius blushed and she wondered if it had something to do with a girl. Her assumption was correct when he said, "The Roshian girl, Helena, lured me out of my room. She tied me up and then the Duke interrogated me. You aren't really going to interrogate me, are you?"

She had to keep him focused or he might just crumble under the emotional pressure of what had been done to him. "Just questions, Demetrius, and quickly. I don't know how long we will have before the Duke figures out how to torture us through the net."

Demetrius winced at the mention of torture but he continued, "He kept asking questions about you and Gideon. Then later he asked about everyone on the ship. I take it that was when you took Hermia away. Is she alright?"

"She is right peachy. She is looking after Angel and keeping herself busy on the Blazing Blunderbuss." Hara reassured him.

"Oh." He seemed almost disappointed that Hermia no longer needed rescuing. Hara wouldn't be surprised if he had dreams of being a daring hero and saving his runaway bride.

"Now, tell me. How many men are there and what is the routine?" Hara got him back on topic by asking him more useful questions.

"Not much of a routine. Some men come in to help me with things and to feed me. I have been in this chair for three days. I can't even feel my ass anymore."

"I can imagine. So no routine? What about men?" Hara wasn't going to let him spend any time feeling sorry for himself. They were in a dangerous place and they needed to stay calm and find a way out of it.

"Well, there were several soldiers who guarded me but I didn't see anyone else. Helena said they left some men in the port as they had to leave quickly. Was that you as well?"

"Talen actually. Don't worry, he can get out of anything. He was supposed to get you out by sneaking in but things got complicated." She hoped he got away. The soldiers left behind were unlikely to do anything rash without direct orders from the Duke if Talen had the bad luck of being caught.

Gideon piped in then. "And a good thing. He wouldn't know about the poison."

"Poison?" Demetrius asked curiously.

Hara answered as she knew Gideon would just rant on about the poison. He had strong feelings about the use of such an indiscriminate weapon. He usually only spoke to her about things like that but she didn't think Gideon was in the mood to be discreet at that moment. "Yes. A poison that can kill dragons. It is supposed to be a secret. Now, do you think you can get those ropes a little loose?"

Gideon lifted his head at the mention of ropes and banged his skull into the back of her head. "Ropes? You know I like ropes."

Hara grumbled at the new bruise. "Not those kinds of ropes."

Demetrius blushed as he quickly got what they meant by ropes. He cleared his throat. "You use ropes?"

Hara rolled her eyes. "Gideon would never let me tie him up." She wasn't about to add that she wasn't interested in being tied up, either. That was just a little too much information for someone she barely knew.

"Sure, I would let you tie me up if I knew you wouldn't leave me there. Oh, and you have to use silk. Have I told you how nice silk rope can be?" Gideon said casually as if they were sitting around the mess table instead of tied up in a dragon hunter net on the airship of a megalomaniac Duke keen on being the next Emperor.

"Shush, this isn't the time to wonder about bed room possibilities." Hara needed to keep them all on task, otherwise, they would never escape.

Demetrius looked embarrassed at their talk. Hara looked around the room again. "The chair isn't bolted. We might get Demetrius down here, where we can help him with his ropes. Now roll." She could feel in the tension of Gideon's body that he was going to add some commentary. She instead elbowed him and counted, "One, two, three." On three, they both rolled.

They crashed against Demetrius' legs. They all yelled out in pain as Demetrius crashed to the ground and sat on top of the two of them. There was a crack of wood and then silence as they tried to work out of their bonds. Demetrius got an arm free and he made a soft sound of triumph. Hara and Gideon only got more tangled in the net rather than escaping themselves. It would be entirely up to Demetrius to get them out before someone came to check on them. Hara should have kept her thoughts to herself.

The door opened. They all looked up, though Hara couldn't see the door from the angle she was trapped in.

Demetrius whispered softly, "Helena." So that was their new visitor.

Hara could see the hope drain from Demetrius' face. The door closed and Helena said, "I'm impressed."

Demetrius firmed his shoulders. He was the only one vaguely free so he was the only one who could fight. Hara knew he understood their predicament as she could see it in the way Demetrius readied himself.

Helena continued, "When I was told that you were resourceful, I didn't believe it."

Hara was curious about the tone of Helena's voice and asked, "Who told you we were resourceful?"

"Marya." Hara swore. She knew that name. She was a Roshian politician who had shot her and left her for dead. Gideon growled as he also recognised the name. Helena didn't seem to notice as she continued, "She told me that under no circumstances were the two of you to be hurt. Apparently, you have some leverage over her.

There is no way she is helping you purely from the goodness of her heart." Hara had to agree with Helena.

Gideon coughed and then reminded Hara. "The diamonds."

That was right. Harlen had told them she had some dirty dealings with some diamond mines. Not that they knew anything more than that but it had been enough to get Marya upset enough to kill Hara. Apparently, Marya had found out more about them and Gideon's links to the Empire as her tune had changed from wanting to kill Hara to now protecting them.

Hara asked, "You can get us out of this?"

"I'll have to. Though I think Marya is undermining her primary project."

Helena crouched down and helped them from the net. Hara said as she waited for the complicated task to be done. "Civil war isn't going to help Rosh. A war will not be contained just within our borders."

"Why not? It has before." Helena grunted as she tugged on the wire cables of the net to release it.

"Gideon, do you want to explain?" Hara and Gideon had long discussions on the political landscape of the Empire. Hara had gotten more interested when she had accidentally stumbled into a Roshian revolution funded by the Roshian government.

"The chances of war spilling over into Rosha if there is a civil war in the Empire is almost 82%."

"What do you mean by almost 82%?" Helena obviously was surprised with the use of mathematical certainty in Gideon's argument.

"Well, it is actually 81.8766% but I find rounding up is quite adequate in situations like this."

Helena gave Gideon a quirky smile. "I'm sure there are many who would say you are more than just adequate, Lord Dragon."

Gideon coughed to hide his surprise at the flirting. Hara came to his rescue. "He is mine."

Gideon didn't dispute her this time and let it lie. Helena finished untying them.

Helena said, "You should be able to fly the two of you away."

Hara asked, "What about you? There is no way the Duke will think we got away out on our own."

Helena quirked an eyebrow and glanced down at the broken chair and ropes on the ground. "You were almost free before."

Hara shook her head. "It is too dangerous to leave you here."

Helena looked at Hara with a strange glow in her eyes. "Why would you help a Roshian spy?"

Gideon answered, "Because she likes people."

Hara snapped. "No, I don't." He made it sound like she collected lost puppies or something because she had a bleeding heart.

Gideon continued, "She also has a soft spot for people who have gotten themselves into trouble that they didn't instigate themselves. Your accent tells me you have been outside of Rosh for a long time."

"Since I was a little girl," Helena admitted.

Demetrius said, "She said she was raised to be a spy."

Gideon nodded. "I have heard of this practice. You really didn't have any choice and you were just a little girl."

Damn, that dragon, but he was right. Hara did like to help people that were like her as a child. A child couldn't know any better. It wasn't like Helena had any choice in being a spy. Just as Hara hadn't had a choice in helping her father con people out of their wealth. She had just been a little girl who had been trying to impress an emotionally distant father who, unfortunately, was a narcissist.

Hara crossed her hands over her chest. "This is the time to choose, Helena. You can remain here and help the Duke play out his plan but you already know that we will deal with him soon. And that the Duke's plan is a sinking ship. You could always go back to your masters and heel like a dog or you can come with us. You will have the freedom to make the choices that you want to make."

"You don't have that power. No one does." Helena accused them incredulously.

Hara tilted her head to indicate Gideon. "He is the great uncle to the Emperor. We might not make it. You can go home but the Emperor owes us a favour and pardoning a spy can be it."

Helena looked at Hara with suspicion. "What do you ask in return? I might have had to do much in the name of Rosh but I am not willing to play the whore just to be free of that master."

Hara frowned and Gideon said, "She thinks you want to sleep with her."

Hara looked shocked. "Oh, never."

Hara blushed and Gideon saved her. "She is mine."

Helena said, "Then what is the price?"

"Help us deal with the Duke. That will burn your bridges with the Roshians and means you have to be with us."

Helena glared at Hara with sharp eyes, then eventually said, "You are shrewd. Yes, I will come with you."

Gideon said, "If you think you can get Marya to back you if you change your mind and want to return to Rosh, then I should tell you the last time we spoke to her. She shot Hara in the chest."

Helena was shocked by this revelation. "Really? Ah, then I really am putting all my eggs in one basket."

Hara nodded her head, happy that they had come to a compromise. She turned to Gideon and asked, "Are you able to carry all of us?"

"Yes, but not for a long distance. But the Blazing Blunderbuss will not be far behind us and we can always land and wait for her to find us," Gideon said hopefully.

Helena said, "Come this way and we must be quiet."

Helena opened the door and looked outside to make sure the way was clear. When it was, she motioned to them to follow her. They had a few hairy moments when they had to duck into an empty room to avoid a few soldiers.

The deck was a mess when they arrived. Hara hadn't realised they had left it in such a state when they had left. There were broken crates and the dolly was on its side. It wasn't like they had resisted their capture.

Gideon said, "They must have searched for the poison."

"Oh." So, it wasn't them that had left the mess. Hara felt a little silly that her instinct was to keep a work space clean.

Gideon said, "I will change and then you guys need to come to the edge of the deck and I will pick you all up in one go. It will be uncomfortable but that is the only way I can guarantee none of you will drop."

Helena asked, "What about riding on your back?"

"Only mates are able to do that," he said in a purr that was incongruent to the situation. Hara would have to ask him about that later but there was something else that bothered her.

Hara asked, "Able?" But before Gideon could answer, Hara felt a bullet enter her shoulder. She cried out and the blow took her to her knees. She put her hand to the wound and felt as it slowly closed under her touch.

Hara watched the Duke who had shot at her step out from the cover of the door. With a yell, Helena threw herself forward to attack him. She knew how to fight better than most men that Hara knew. She moved fast, a knife in her hand, jabbing in at the Duke trying to cut at his middle. The Duke might have looked like a dandy to rival Demetrius but he could fight. He disarmed Helena of her knife and buried her own blade into her leg without even losing his own gun. He kicked her away with disdain marring his features.

Helena landed on her backside and scrambled away from the Duke. Hara went for a net ball and was waiting for the Duke to lower his weapon so he wouldn't shoot one of them again. The next time might be more fatal.

The Duke saw her tall stance. "You recover well, I see. The immortality of dragons is not just a myth and can be passed on to someone in their collection." He walked closer to them as he spoke. He eyed Hara with a lusty look but Hara didn't think he was thinking of sex at all.

He was getting closer and Hara was worried that he would not drop his guard long enough for any of them to deal with him.

The Duke moved fast. He yanked on the hand that was holding the net ball and twisted it around behind Hara's back when he was close enough. Hara yelped in pain.

When the others tried to attack, the Duke waved the gun. "Ah, not so quickly. I know you can kill a human in a collection. It is a slow process, though." He licked her cheek, though she knew he was only doing that to unsettle Gideon. Lysander purred. "My bastard of a father would roll in his grave if he knew I was immortal. His sin and mistake living forever would be the ultimate punishment for what he did to me, his own flesh and blood. Regardless that he didn't marry my mother, he should have given me the same rights as any of his sons."

Gideon said, "You want to be in my collection. You want to be immortal. Let her go and I will give you this gift."

Hara tried to wriggle free but the position she was in was painful and the bullet wound in her shoulder hadn't completely healed. Gideon made a move and the Duke quickly placed the barrel of the gun against her head. Everyone went still. Gideon's voice got very cold. He didn't talk like this very often and when he did, people ignored him at their peril.

"You are not to hurt her." Gideon's voice was more than fierce, it was vicious.

The Duke said, "I won't need to as long as you agree to make me immortal. I will be the Emperor of the Empire forever." He giggled at the end, giddy to be an immortal ruler.

Helena gasped out in pain as she got to her feet. She gritted her teeth and yanked out the blade. She said through her teeth, "You are a fool Lysander."

The Duke turned his attention to Helena. "Says the little chit who thought no one realised she was a bloody whore as well as a spy. You were a good lay though while it lasted."

Helena surged forward and the Duke automatically turned his gun towards her. Before he could pull the trigger though Gideon charged him. The Duke let Hara go and Gideon changed his trajectory and instead went for her. Together with Gideon, they went over the edge of the dock and off the airship.

Gideon changed into a dragon and with amazing dexterity, shifted her to his shoulder. She caught hold of the mane that swept down his back. Hara called out, though her words were whipped away by the wind when she saw two other tumbling objects fall out of the sky.

Gideon must have seen them himself as he dived and caught the two bodies. Hara prayed they were still alive. It surely hadn't been long enough for the Duke to shoot them and shove them over the edge. But she had been concentrating on falling rather than on how much time had passed.

⸺⸺⸺⸺⸺⸺⸺⸺⸺⸺

Gideon's prediction that the Blazing Blunderbuss wasn't very far away was correct. Gideon dropped Helena and Demetrius on the deck before he grabbed hold of the railing. Helena and Demetrius were shivering and struggling to get to their feet but very much alive.

Hara climbed over Gideon and onto the solid wood of the deck. Gideon changed and rolled onto the deck.

Hara swore. He was bleeding from his shoulder. The Duke must have hit him with a stray bullet when Gideon had charged him.

Hara slipped an arm under his and helped him to his room. He rolled onto the bed and Hara asked, "Should I get Hermia in here to see if her stitching is any better than mine."

Gideon shook his head. His eyes closed with pain. "No need. It will close up soon."

She wasn't so sure of that. The wound was still bleeding sluggishly. She pulled a chair over and sat next to the bed. She was contemplating getting some water and cleaning him up when the bleeding stopped. Maybe it had been the flying that had kept the wound open for so long.

Hara touched her own shoulder. That was almost completely healed. She said, more to herself than Gideon. "I'm immortal."

Gideon opened his eyes. "Maybe. We haven't established yet the parameters that will mean we will live forever."

Hara shook her head. "But you think dragons are immortal but what does that mean for me?"

"Remember once I told you about how all the little tiny stuff that is inside of me that came here through nothing and joined with all the little tiny stuff that is you." Hara only vaguely remembered that conversation. He had tried to explain how dragons had come from their original planet by tangling their small bits with people's small bits and that is why they looked like humans when they shifted.

"Yes, you called it entanglement or something. I didn't understand it but you mean because of that I will have the same life span as you."

"Yes. While my matter remains in this form, you will live as long as I do. Dragons do die but now that we are at peace with humans, it is rare."

Hara contemplated that concept for a moment and asked, "Is that why the Emperors only stay on the throne for fifty years. Are the others still alive?"

"Most of them. There was one who killed himself doing something daring but the others are still alive." His voice wasn't as pained as it had been a moment before.

"Not all of them were mated to dragons. In fact, none of them were," Hara said, confused on how they could all live so long when they weren't purely dragons.

"Hybrid dragons are different. They seem to have the same longevity we had on our home planet. Which is about a thousand years. The Empire is only six hundred years old so we have seen the hybrids grow older but not die yet."

"William? William the conqueror is still alive." Hara asked about the first hybrid who had started the Empire at the start of the millennium.

"No, he was the one who killed himself doing something daring. He had too much dragon blood in him, in any case. He wanted to collect the whole world. And that would have ended badly."

Hara leant back in the chair. "So, I'm related to dragons and now I'm practically royalty."

"I wouldn't call being royalty practical," Gideon said with a smile in his voice.

"It is if I can rescue a Roshian spy."

Gideon chuckled, but closed his eyes on the pain it caused. Hara couldn't imagine him flying with that wound for the hours it had taken them to find the Blazing Blunderbuss.

She placed her hand on his uninjured shoulder. "I'll go get you some food and check on the others. Then we need to do something about the Duke." She got up to leave.

Before she could leave the room, Gideon asked, "Will you fly with me again?"

Hara had her hand on the door handle and stopped to turn to look at him. His eyes were open and the gold seemed bright at that moment.

She said, "Yes."

He smiled. "Good. That means I'm finally yours."

"Is it a trust thing?" She had been wondering why only mates could ride on the backs of dragons.

He shook his head. "Partly. But more about intimacy."

She was shocked by this answer. "Intimacy?"

He smiled and closed his eyes, but not in pain. "Mmm, you see when dragon's mate, they entwine together in the air. We can't do that with our human mates but flying as we did gets pretty close."

Hara was tempted to throw something at his head and instead resisted the urge and just slammed the door as she left.

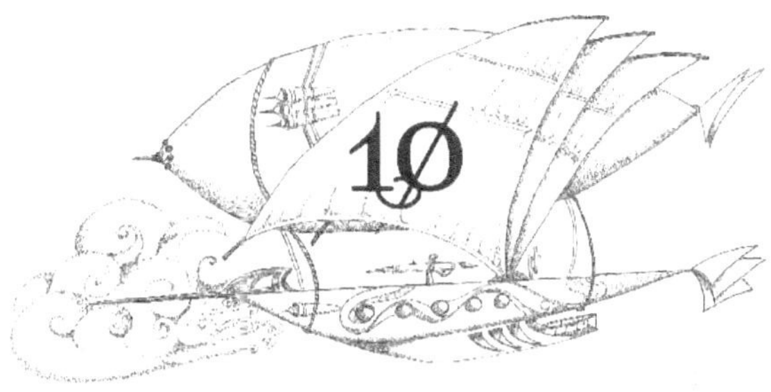

emetrius was looking a lot better. Hara had been worried the flight would have made his wounds worse but it seemed some good food and some rest was all he really needed. He was still a mottled paint pot of colours as his bruises slowly healed. Hara almost felt guilty as the wound in her shoulder from the bullet was already completely healed.

Helena was limping but was otherwise very mobile. The crew eyed her with suspicion but didn't question why she was sitting at the mess table along with the others.

Hara stood at the head of the table and waited for everyone to settle down. She might be the Captain of the Blazing Blunderbuss often worked as a dictatorship but Hara couldn't take them to fight a war without their input. Hara started from the beginning as she had no idea how much the others had gossiped about.

"Duke Lysander is getting ready to go to war with the Empire. We are not all friends of the Empire but they are willing to give us a pardon if we do the Emperor a favour."

Murphy butted in. "I thought we only had to get the girl." He pointed at Hermia. "And we have her. Why can't we mosey back to the Empire, drop the girl off and run far away?"

Liam said, "I'm surprised, Murphy. You are usually the one wanting to get into a fight."

"Not a fight that is likely to get me killed," he added in a practical tone, not even slightly offended by Liam's accusations.

Hara had to agree with Murphy but there was more to the situation than he knew. "It is true that this is dangerous but I don't think there is much choice. You see, the problem is bigger than you might be aware of. Lysander is planning to start a civil war and the Roshians want to take advantage of the infighting to nibble at the edges of the Empire. This is a boiling pot and it is going to throw the whole continent into war."

Murphy shrugged. "Then let us head over to the nearest Empire fort and tell them they have a problem and let them rout out the bugger and we don't have to risk our necks."

There was a tense silence after that. Eventually, Hara said when it was clear that no one was going to interrupt with their own thoughts, "We could do that, but the fort is unlikely to attack one of their lords on our say so. We are still pirates in their eyes and we could talk till we are blue in our face before they will believe us."

Murphy was obviously in a perverse mood as he said, "Get Gideon to order them around. He is a dragon. Surely they will listen to a dragon."

Hermia actually spoke up. "The Empire nobility doesn't work like that. A dragon can't just walk into a place and give orders to the army. The Emperor would never allow that."

Murphy sulked and went silent after that. Hara continued. "So that means we can't go to the Empire army and I'm going to explain why we can't just leave Lysander to wander around without someone stopping him. You remember that crazy scientist we transported last year who supposedly fell off the ship and died?"

Liam groaned. "He was a complete nutter."

Hara nodded, agreeing with him. "Well, he was taken by the Empire and put into a secret lab where he could work for the Empire instead of against it. But the problem is that someone got to him and the recipe for the poison he had made."

Murphy asked, "What poison?"

Hara flushed as she had forgotten that she and Gideon had kept that part under their hats. "Ah, well, the crazy scientist figured out a poison to kill dragons."

Helena slapped the table. "That is why he got so cocky about two weeks ago. Lysander must have gotten the recipe." Then Helena's face got dark. "You are right then, Captain, we do have to take him down. The dragons used to be invaders to this world but they are now an important part of this world. Without them, our society would fall apart." When people looked at her in surprise, she said, "I read."

Hermia said, "She is right. Our science and industry is vastly influenced by dragons. If they disappeared overnight, we would be thrown into anarchy."

There was a tangible silence as everyone took it in. Hara said, "So I know you aren't keen to get bloody but we just might have to."

Liam clapped his hands as he said excitedly, "I know."

When everyone turned to him, he looked surprised. Hara wondered if he realised he had spoken out loud. He flushed pink on his cheeks. "I know how to deal with the automata. Once they are engaged, then the normal soldiers should be called to reinforce them. That will leave the castle mostly empty. We can go in and take on the main players. Once they are out, we can leave. The soldiers will go back to being soldiers to someone else. Hopefully, someone not keen on being the next emperor."

Hara looked at everyone's faces. They all seemed surprised by Liam's outburst. Gideon grinned. "Good on you, boy. I think that is brilliant. Now, who are the players who need to be eliminated and who needs to be distracted?"

<hr>

Demetrius followed Hermia when she left the mess hall. He wanted to catch her by herself.

He called, "Hermia!"

She turned but before he could say anything, Helena limped out of the mess. She nodded her head to the two of them and disappeared further into the ship. Demetrius' watched her as she left. He couldn't believe the courage she had shown to turn on her own people and join them, even though it was the right thing to do.

Demetrius could hardly find the courage to stand up to his own parents, let alone a whole country.

Hermia asked, "What do you want, Demetrius?"

He blinked as he brought his mind to the conversation he wanted to have with Hermia. He had planned what he would say to convince her to spend time with him.

When he opened his mouth, a whole other conversation came out. "I'm glad you ran away."

He blushed when he realised he wasn't being very tactful. Hermia just looked at him so he rushed on. "I mean, you are right. We aren't suited for each other. My parents were putting a lot of pressure on me to marry. I should have found out if you were keen before I caved. I'm sorry that you were the one who had to act and that it brought us all to this. If I had a bit more backbone when it comes to my parents, we could have avoided all of this."

Hermia blinked and he wondered if she had understood what he had said. Before he could think of something else to say which would probably make him sound more like an idiot, Hermia said, "It wasn't your fault, Demetrius. It was Lysander's. He was the one that convinced me I shouldn't marry you. But I think you are right. We aren't suited. I don't want to marry at the moment. I think I might travel for a bit."

She patted his shoulder and then sauntered away. Demetrius still wasn't sure what had just happened. Murphy said from the corridor behind him, "Girls."

Demetrius turned and Murphy patted him on his shoulder in sympathy. At least he wasn't the only one who had been confused in the sudden change in that conversation.

❖————————————————❖

Once everyone had left the room, Hara was left with Angel and Gideon. He was still seated at the table playing with Angel and the nuts she was counting on the table.

He said without looking up at her, "Thank you."

Hara frowned. "For what?"

Gideon turned to look at her. "For risking your life to go after this man."

Hara shrugged. "I think it is stupidity. You do know that even if we take him down and Puck that it still won't change that they gave the recipe for the poison to someone outside of the Empire. It will get out eventually, no matter what you do."

135

"I know and I will see if Harlen can track down the party outside of the Empire. We might have a few more years if he had stalled that leak."

Hara sat down next to him and stole some of Angel's nuts until she chittered and the two of them played tug of war with a nut.

Hara didn't look at Gideon as she said, "I don't know if gaining time will solve the problem."

Gideon sat back and watched the two of them. "With time, we can come up with an inoculation or an antidote. I'm not a doctor but I have talked to Harlen about it. He likes medicine more than I do and he says that within a decade they will have a way to combat the poison. We just have to stall for that long. We know you can't keep secrets forever."

Angel finally got all the nuts and Hara turned to Gideon. "What about the traitor?"

He frowned and said sadly, "That is something I will deal with."

Hara raised an eyebrow. "You already know who it is." It wasn't a question.

Hara didn't want to even contemplate what he was feeling. To find out that one of your kind was willing to risk all of them for some sort of power play against those who had found some happiness on this planet. Dragons were an endangered species and they were all male on this planet. Without this bonding with humans, they would have been an extinct race just waiting to die.

Hara said, "Your kind is an endangered species. I can't imagine what would have to go through someone's mind to contemplate the genocide of almost your entire race." She shook her head, grieving lives that weren't even lost yet.

Hara asked as the thought occurred to her. "Will I die if you do because of the bonding?"

"Most likely not straight away but you wouldn't have the same healing powers you do now and that is not acceptable." Hara also realised that Gideon would have very little mercy for whoever was the dragon traitor. Hara added, "Just make sure that whatever you do about the traitor that it sits right with you. This is not a time to be rash."

<hr>

Demetrius knew he should try to get some sleep. As they would arrive at the castle, the next day and they would need all their wits about them. But there was a nervous energy in Demetrius that made it impossible to sleep. Near midnight, he thought he would try something else besides tossing in his bed.

He went to the mess. He expected it to be empty but Helena was there with Angel. Angel was playing a shell game with Helena and trying to guess which cup the nut was under. Angel tapped a cup and Helena lifted it up to reveal the nut underneath. Angel chittered excitedly and clicked her claws together.

Demetrius watched them for a moment. He had thought he was quiet enough that Helena wasn't aware of him but she said without looking up from the cups. "You can come in. I won't bite." She turned to look at him. "Only if you want me to."

Demetrius said, "You don't have to flirt with me, you know."

Her eyes were hurt and he wondered what he had said to offend her. She said softly, "I'm sorry you were hurt. I have done some horrible things in my life but I really hate it when innocents are hurt. There was no reason for the Duke to take you. We knew you wouldn't know a lot but I think he wanted revenge because the Emperor somehow thought you would make a better groom than him."

Demetrius snorted. "That is because I am nobody. I am the third son. There is no way I'm going to be anything important."

Helena seemed surprised. "I thought you were the oldest. Why would the Empire bother with a third son?"

Demetrius shrugged. "I have good blood, that is all. But I've already told Hermia that I can't marry her. She was right, we don't suit and we would make each other miserable and that is not a nice thing to do to your spouse."

Helena raised an eyebrow. "Why doesn't she suit? You have barely spent any time together."

He sighed. "It is because I think I'm looking for someone who makes me into a better person. She is lovely but she doesn't inspire me to be the person I want to be."

Helena smiled. "Maybe one day you can marry for love and find that person who inspires you to be better. I wish I could find that person. All I've had in my life is people who want to use me instead of seeing what potential I can achieve because they believe in me." Helena got to her feet and approached him. She kissed him on the cheek. "If it counts, you are my hero. After all, you rescued me."

Demetrius frowned. "How did I do that?"

Helena just gave him an enigmatic smile and left the mess. Angel chittered a question and Demetrius said as he watched Helena walk away. "I don't know, Angel. I really don't know."

They all were in the cargo bay. Liam was fiddling with some powders and muttering to himself. Murphy was checking his weapons while the others stood around nervously.

Hara said, "Gideon and I will deal with the army. Henry and Murphy are going to run the ship and use the guns. They are the ones who don't mind a bit of blood on their hands and it is going to be bloody dealing with that army."

She paused but no one disagreed. "Alice, Angel, Talen and Hermia will go after Lysander. Hermia, Lysander will get distracted when he sees you as he is obsessed with his bid for the throne and it will seem his answers are there in human form. Talen is to deal with him. Alice and Angel, you are to make sure that Hermia makes it back alive. The Emperor will not want us to get her killed. Understood?" It was a risk to send Hermia but Hara had already seen Lysander fight and she didn't think any of them were his equal. Not unless they could make him fight emotionally.

Angel sat on Alice's shoulder and tightened her claws in her hair, making Alice wince but she nodded her head. Hara didn't need to look at Talen. He was a thief and a scoundrel. He had his own share of blood on his hands.

Hara turned to the others. "Helena, Demetrius and Liam, you are to go after Puck."

Liam asked, "Don't you need me to help you with the devices?"

Hara shook her head. "You have done a good job and they will give us the advantage, but Demetrius is not a trained fighter. He might need some help."

Demetrius took offence to that. "Hey."

Helena said, "She is right. Liam and I can both fight dirty. Do you want us to kill the engineer?" The last was directed to Hara.

"Only if you have to. The Empire will have a nice lab hidden away for him if he is willing to trade employers. He is too dangerous to leave free though so if he doesn't agree, then you might have to kill him." Helena was like Talen in that she had her own share of blood on her hands, but Hara had seen how quickly the girl had grasped a chance to be a normal person. Hara didn't want to sabotage the changes the girl was already instigating in herself. But Puck was also very dangerous as he knew the secret to killing off an entire race and no one should have that knowledge.

Puck was a scientist so she hoped he would take the logical path but she had also wondered if he was possessed by the same obsession as Lysander.

"Now Liam before you go, show us again what surprises you have planned for Lysander's automata army."

Liam motioned them over to powders he had been playing with. "I left some out so you could see how it works. Be careful because if some of it spills, we will set the whole ship on fire."

He put a little of each powder into a small crucible and then a thin wire.

He said as he worked, "I've set this into mines. They attach to the metal of the automata and you light it from a fuse. Gideon can probably just blow some fire towards it once it is set. It will take a while for it to take effect so you will need to move fast."

Gideon said, "No problem."

Liam set the wire on fire and it burnt like an oil-soaked rag and then there was a bright flash and sparks flew. Murphy went to stamp out the sparks but Liam stopped him and instead said, "Not to worry, I put down a plate to catch the sparks." The reaction settled but everyone could feel the heat radiating off the glowing crucible.

Everyone flinched except Liam. "I heard of this stuff from some pirates in that port we were wintering this year. Apparently, the Han have all sorts of things that burn like this. This is hot. Hotter than a furnace and should melt the metal. So don't get near it as it burns," Liam explained.

Hara was surprised by how long it burned. She looked at Liam with pride. "You are more than my apprentice now. You are your own master now. This is brilliant."

Gideon said, "Mmm. Interesting."

Hara glanced at his underwhelmed tone, "You know what this is?"

"You would call it thermite and I have heard of it. We even used it on our own planet. It is useful for cutting metal as it melts directly down. The men inside the automata will be injured by this."

Liam pursed his lips for a moment. "They will most likely be killed. Gideon. I know what this means."

Hara blinked in confusion. She looked at Gideon but thought she would talk to him later. She was glad that they were going to be the ones who would use these weapons. At least she could spare Liam seeing the burnt corpses of the men killed inside the automata.

She patted Liam on his shoulder. "Well, people, let us invade a castle."

11

It was clear the Duke was expecting them. Hara stood on the bridge with Henry. He was going to do the flying, even though Alice would have probably done a better job. But Hara had felt that Henry wasn't as invested in the airship as he used to be.

She said as she watched the automata file out of the castle and range themselves around the walls of the castle. "You are going to move on, aren't you?"

When there was only silence, she turned to look at Henry. He was flushed and he coughed to clear something in his throat before he answered, "I didn't realise you had figured it out. I'm ready to settle down but I will see this through. I miss living in the Empire. While the only options I had were living in some backwater-middle-of-nowhere town, I wasn't keen to leave but I want to go home."

Hara nodded. "I understand. We will miss you."

Gideon came onto the deck. He was only wearing a pair of slacks. She looked at his fine chest. He really was a good-looking man. She turned to look at the automata again so she wouldn't show the tinge of pink to her cheeks.

He looked down at the automata. "This is going to be close. Are you still sure?"

Hara was surprised he had asked. She turned to him and caught up his hands. "I thought you knew me, Gideon. I can't leave these people to be around to hurt people."

"Mostly dragons," he countered.

Hara shook her heads denying his words. "They are people as well. You didn't come here because you wanted a holiday. You came here because you were desperate. To turn your people away because you scare us is small-minded."

Gideon tightened his hands around her own. "Mine."

Hara slowly smiled and returned. "Mine."

He nodded decisively. "Time to go make a mess and start some mayhem."

Murphy walked in to the gun station, heard the last and said, "Hoorah."

The rest on the bridge also said, "Hoorah."

Hara followed Gideon when he left the bridge. She was in as much armour as she could manage but she had opted for leather rather than metal. They would need speed and agility more than protection. She had several bags of the devices Liam had made. She hoped she wouldn't need them all as he had made almost a hundred of the small compact bombs.

Gideon stopped when they got to the deck. "I have transported the saddle here."

Hara asked, "Saddle?"

She knew Gideon had access to his collection no matter where he was. It was some trick similar to the one that had transported his people from another planet completely. He had admitted it was mostly made up of books and money. She hadn't realised he had kept other things.

"Yeah. I'm going to be moving fast and I don't want to lose you. You will need to buckle yourself in, otherwise it will be dangerous." He motioned to a contraption in the shadows. "Throw it over the side when I change and I'll put it on. Then jump with all your gear. You'll be able to strap it on and yourself."

This already sounded better. Hara had wondered how she would hold on to Gideon and the bags and set them on the automata. This way, she would have her hands free.

Gideon stepped off backwards off the deck while blowing her a kiss. Hara blew a kiss back, even though he wouldn't be able to see.

She lugged the saddle over the edge, surprised by how heavy it was. She picked up the sacks of bombs next and looked over the edge. Gideon was flitting around and she could see the saddle already on his back. Dragons were a hell of a lot more agile than she had realised. She whistled and then stepped off the edge. This time differed from when Gideon had taken her over the edge to get her away from Lysander.

Her heart leapt into her throat. Then Gideon was catching her and slipped her onto his back. There were a few straps and she first tied down the bags before she strapped in her legs. It was a tight fit but she also didn't have to worry about falling out.

Gideon banked sharply and she clutched at his mane, even though she was already safely strapped in. She saw the large fire ball flying. So that was the reason for the sudden manoeuvre.

They would have to deal with the catapult first as it could also attack the air ship. Gideon was fast enough that he could avoid it. Well, it was off to war.

Helena had known of some secret passageways or they would never have gotten into the castle. Once inside, they had parted into their two groups. Helena took point but Demetrius wasn't going to argue over it. She clearly had more skills in this arena than he did.

Liam said behind him in a soft voice, "She is a fine woman."

Demetrius glanced over his shoulder, surprised by the young man's words. He raised an eyebrow for Liam to elaborate.

He must have understood as Liam said, "Smart, good looking and she can kick some serious ass."

Demetrius looked back at Helena. She had already taken out a few soldiers who had been protecting the secret tunnels. She hadn't even broken a sweat.

Helena said without looking back, "You two keep it down." She motioned them to follow her as she ducked down a corridor.

Helena was also on point because she knew where Puck's lab was. Hara had said they had found it but hadn't known how to get there from the secret tunnels.

Helena suddenly ran and Demetrius realised there were two guards outside Puck's lab. Demetrius rushed to help her but she had already disabled one and was engaged with the other. Demetrius watched her with awe.

Liam said, "One awesome lady."

Helena finished with her man and said to Liam, "Thanks for the compliment. Now be careful. The engineer will have something planned for us."

Liam grinned. "So do I."

Liam stepped up to the door. He took a few things out of his pocket and opened his canteen. He poured water over the balls and they bubbled. He then crouched and rolled the small balls under the door and stood up.

Helena frowned and asked, "What was that?"

"Gas in small balls. They will react to the water I just poured on them and fill the area around the door with smoke and gas. We should be able to go through soon."

Liam then stepped back and gave the door a hearty kick, which slammed it open. Helena rushed in through the smoke.

Demetrius looked at Liam. "You are full of surprises."

Liam grinned wider. "I learnt from the best."

Liam pulled out two guns and followed Helena. Demetrius, not to be outdone, also rushed into the room. There was only one light left in the large cavernous room, making it hard to make out anything. There were screams and yells so Demetrius knew there were more men in the room than just the engineer. Demetrius stayed near the door where the light came in from the corridor so they could see if anyone tried to escape.

A man dashed forward and Demetrius kicked out his leg, taking the man in the gut. He went down with an oomph and Demetrius danced on his feet, feeling the adrenaline from taking down his first man.

Helena yelled. "Down!"

Demetrius wasn't sure who she was talking to so he shifted aside. He jumped when he realised someone had come up behind him. He fumbled with his gun in its holster but before he could even bring it up; the man grew a knife in his throat. The surprise on the man's face was grotesque as blood spurted out of the wound on his neck. Demetrius glanced over his shoulder to briefly glimpse Helena in the light with her hand now empty of a knife. But she moved back into the shadows, fighting other men.

Demetrius turned back to the man, who had now slumped to the floor. Helena had just saved his life. How was he supposed to be the hero when Helena was always saving him?

<hr>

Hermia listened to Alice as she asked Talen, "Why do you not trust Gideon with Hara?"

Talen glanced back disapproving. Hermia wasn't sure if that was because they were talking while they were supposed to be sneaking through the castle or because he didn't like the question.

He said softly, "It is none of your business."

Alice snorted at that concept. "Hara is my captain and she is my friend. Gideon is my friend as well. He has treated me very well. He knows my history and yet he hasn't given me any trouble about it. Not like you."

Talen turned again to glare at Alice. Hermia didn't know what incident Alice was talking about but Talen had been surly the entire time she had known him so she wouldn't be surprised if he had offended Alice at some stage. "I thought you could do with the company. It isn't like there is anything of quality for you to choose from," he hissed back softly.

Alice said, "The fact that you think I have to choose is the problem, Talen, but you are avoiding the issue. What is it about Gideon that annoys you?"

There was a long silence as they made their way through the corridors of the castle, where Hermia thought Talen wouldn't answer at all.

Eventually, he said, 'He isn't good enough for her."

Alice huffed. "That shows what you know. You do know that he is related to the Emperor. He is rich and he is smart. Also, he treats her like she is royalty. You are just saying that because you really can't find anything about him that is wrong."

"He is an arrogant ass. He thinks he knows everything but he knows jack." He snapped a little louder than he had before.

"Unlike you, who have spent only a few short years on this planet, you think you can know more than him. He actually knows more than you realise. He usually keeps it all to himself because it would baffle us."

"How do you know all this? Is Gideon cheating on Hara with you?" Talen motioned for them to be silent and to stop. They moved back to a room and closed the door. They waited a while for whoever had been outside to move past them.

But Alice wasn't about to be distracted from her conversation and she asked, "No, I'm not sleeping with Gideon. And you are an idiot on two counts for thinking that. First that he would do something like that and secondly that I would do something like that to Hara. No, he talks to Hara on the bridge while I'm there. The two of them talk about the universe and all sorts of crazy intelligent stuff. You never hear any of that because you are too busy sulking with Murphy."

"I'm not sulking." There was a long silence and Hermia thought Alice was right not to argue that point as his childish tone was all that was needed. Besides, they were getting to a part of the castle which was more populated.

Talen signalled they could move from the room. When they got to a junction, Talen was about to go towards the front of the castle.

Hermia said, "This way."

She pointed to the large doors that opened to the library. Talen asked, "What is in there?"

Hermia smiled. "Something that will suit you, Talen. Treasure. The Duke has a vault in there."

Alice asked with awe in her voice, "How did you find that out?"

Hermia shrugged it off. "I go in there a lot and there are some places where I can hide and no one knows I'm there. Once I knew the Duke was rotten, I thought I would spy on him. He was in there one day when he thought I was somewhere else and there was a vault behind some books. If we can get his wealth away from Lysander, then we won't have to kill him but he won't be a problem to the Empire."

Talen agreed as he said, "No gold, no army."

"Exactly." Hermia smiled, pleased with her alternative to killing. She wasn't entirely comfortable with bloodshed but she was happy to cause some mayhem in Lysander's life.

Inside the library, Hermia showed them to the wall. "I'm not sure how to get in. I only know it is behind here."

Talen dusted off his hands. "Not to worry, sister, this is where my talents shine."

Hermia went to stand with Alice where they could watch Talen and the door together. Talen moved along the wall, tapping and moving things. It didn't take him long to find something that was out of place and he moved some books aside to reveal a combination lock hidden behind them.

Talen motioned at them to be quiet and Hermia and Alice stood in silence.

Angel crawled to the top of Alice's head to get a better view of what Talen was doing and Alice winced as the creature must have pulled her hair in the attempt.

Hermia was fascinated with the small creature. It was not a machine in her eyes. She had seen enough of the automata around the Duke's castle to know that they were a far cry from the delicate creature that was full of personality and sentience that was Angel. Angel reminded Hermia more of a pet than a machine.

There was a click and Talen opened the wall that was the door to the vault. There was a small room on the other side, which was mostly empty. There were two chests of gold and Talen went to that. He lifted one with a grunt and motioned with his head for them to get the other.

Hermia stepped forward but Alice waved for her to stand back. Hermia wondered if it was because she was a noblewoman but then Alice had a bit more muscle than her.

<hr>

The molten body of one automata creaked and then tumbled over, taking one of his fellow mechanicals with him. Hara held onto the saddle with one hand as Gideon spun in the air away from the hot sparks coming from the thermite mine.

If Hara was even a little bit affected by motion sickness, she would have found this intolerable. But since the erratic movement meant they could avoid the last catapult, Hara wasn't going to complain.

As they straightened out, Hara could see the battlefield a bit better. The Blazing Blunderbuss was behind the west tower and was engaged with the soldiers on the wall. Hara could hear the rat-a-tat of the guns as

Murphy returned their fire. Though she doubted he actually hit anything. The gunfire alone meant that the soldiers were forced to take cover. The front of the castle was another thing.

The Blazing Blunderbuss had thrown a steel net over one automata and it was still wriggling and trying to break free. Hara doubted there was a punch card that had the instructions to do that and the man trapped inside would have to wait until later to be freed.

There was a small huddle of automata which they had hit early on. Their heads and shoulders melted from the thermite.

There were others like this but they were mostly singular as the automata had gotten wise to their attacks and avoided most of them. Lysander was on the wall now and Hara could hear him yelling.

The gates surged open and other creatures shaped more like ants and spiders came scuttling out. They had soldiers riding on their backs in metal cages. Hara shook her head. They would have been an advantage against foot soldiers but not against a dragon. They were too exposed in the cages to avoid Gideon's fire. It was going to be a slaughter. But Hara didn't feel sorry for the soldiers. They were the ones who had signed on with a Duke who was clearly mad. If she had been one of those soldiers, she would have ducked off somewhere no matter how much she was called a coward. Fighting for crazy was never good for the health.

⋯⋯⋯

A bright flash illuminated the lab as one table further back caught alight. Demetrius, who had been fighting with a soldier, stumbled back. The soldier took advantage and cut his arm. Demetrius had disarmed the soldier of his gun already so the long knife was his only weapon. The pain in Demetrius' arm reminded him that even a knife was deadly enough to kill him.

Before the soldier could do more, Liam moved up behind the soldier and smashed something over his head. A liquid sluiced the man. The soldier turned on Liam but Liam was already lighting a match. The soldier frowned, then realised that the jar smashed over his head had contained oil. Liam grinned and lifted the lit match.

The soldier didn't even fight he just ran. Liam said to Demetrius, "That looks like all of them."

Helena said, "Not all of them." She pointed.

At the door where the soldier had disappeared was Puck. He glared at them. So much for the man being in his lab. Demetrius didn't wait for the others he attacked as he was the closest to the door.

Puck stumbled backwards out of the door at the attack and slipped on the oil. He cracked his head on the stone as he went down.

Demetrius tried to halt his own forward momentum but he slipped on the oil and he went down, crashing into the engineer. Demetrius quickly found his feet, not wanting to be close enough to the engineer that he could kill him with whatever weapon he had. But Puck didn't move. Liam came to stand in the door and nudged the engineer's foot with his own and still the man didn't move.

Helena pushed past Liam and crouched down by the engineer and felt for a pulse. Demetrius held his breath and when Helena looked up and shook her head, Demetrius finally let it out. Demetrius hadn't liked the idea of killing the engineer. He had thought he was a strange man on the airship but Demetrius had known him. Had sat down and had a meal with him.

The other soldiers they had fought had known they were risking their lives when they became soldiers and Demetrius didn't know any of them, so killing them didn't come with the same mix of confusing emotions. Demetrius had actually liked the idea of convincing the man to work for the Empire, even though he had been pretty sure Puck wouldn't have gone for that particular plan.

Helena closed the engineer's eyes. "That will give Gideon some peace of mind."

Demetrius wasn't so sure. The engineer had told at least one other person about the poison. There could have been others. Also, now they couldn't question him about who he had told. Or who had given him the information in the first place?

As only a traitor close to the Emperor could have known about the poison, let alone have access to the scientist himself. Hara had explained how the scientist was thought to be dead by the rest of the world so he wasn't even allowed to wander around. Gideon had assured all of them the scientist was so obsessed with his work, he didn't mind. Puck, on the other hand seemed a man who liked his adventures. He would have withered away in a lab like that.

<hr>

Getting the gold was enough to deal with Lysander so they needed to get out of the castle but without anyone seeing them. It meant that Hermia was on point, as she knew the castle better than anyone else. Hermia opened the door as the other two were weighed down with the loot they had taken from the vault.

Hermia stumbled back as there were soldiers on the other side. They were just as surprised to see her as she was to see them but they recovered quickly. One grabbed her arm while the soldiers went to fight the others.

Angel jumped from Alice's shoulder and spat needles at the men. There were cries of pain but Hermia couldn't see who it was coming from as the soldier had shoved her up against the wall. He pulled her arm behind her back and shoved her down the corridor away from the fight.

Hermia struggled until the soldier slid out a blade and placed it on her shoulder by her neck. She went still after that and let the soldier take her where he wanted. Where that was, was on the walls of the castle.

Lysander yelled out orders on the walls and men were scrambling around him. Hermia could see that there was chaos on the ground below them. Hara and Gideon were making a decent dent in the castle's automata as Lysander look flustered. When Lysander saw her, his eyes shone with an unnatural glow. Apparently Hara had been correct in assuming he would let his obsession focus on her.

Lysander grabbed her and pulled her away from the soldier. The move was such a surprise that the soldier accidentally cut her chin with the knife.

Lysander ignored this and yelled at the soldier who had brought her. "Get the priest. The one in the tower."

The soldier merely nodded his head and went off to comply. Lysander shoved her down, so she was forced onto her knees. He apparently liked her down there as he grinned viciously. "You have cost me a lot, little Hermia but we are about to make that all worth it. With you as my bride, I will have the resources to double my army and I will still be able to be the next emperor." He waved to the mayhem below. "This is all just a mere setback."

When Hermia tried to get to her feet, he shoved her down again and motioned to one of his men and commanded. "Give me your knife."

The soldier glanced at Hermia but he didn't say anything and slid his knife out of the sheath on his leg and handed it to the Duke. The soldier then went back to firing at the dragon with his rifle.

Lysander placed the blade just under her chin. "You will marry me, my dear. I swear I will be a better husband to you than that silly boy, Demetrius. He cried so when I tortured him."

Hermia lifted her chin and firmed her jaw. She wasn't going to spur on his rant by giving him any fuel. She would wait for her opportunity.

Lysander leant forward and he spat a little with the passion he spoke with. "You will be an Empress, my dear. That is a gift that boy could never have given you. He was destined to be a harbour master at best."

Again, Hermia ignored his words. Lysander raised an eyebrow. "So stoic, my dear. Don't you have something to say?"

Hermia let the smile touch her lips briefly before she said, "I have a lot to say, Lysander. I say that I will never marry a conceited ass like you. You would have to be burning in hell before I would even spit on you to put you out."

Lysander didn't like her words as his face twisted up with anger. Before he could say anything, the soldier returned with the priest.

Lysander turned to the priest. "You are to marry us. Now!"

The priest looked between her and Lysander. "I am only to marry those who wish it."

Lysander lifted the knife from her throat to threaten the priest. "You will marry us or I will gut you where you stand. Do you understand?"

The priest looked at her. Lysander was a fool. This was a marriage under duress. There was no one that would make her stay married to Lysander. All she had to do was walk out on him. She had left the castle once she could do it again. She nodded slightly to the priest to go ahead and not to risk his life.

The priest pursed his lips and said to Lysander, "I will do as you ask but it will not serve you well. The church is powerful and they do not look kindly on threats."

Lysander dropped his knife to his side, pleased that the priest was going to comply. Hermia watched the knife rather than the priest. She was just waiting for her chance.

Lysander said, "It matters not what the church thinks, priest, as long as we are married."

Lysander turned to deal with her but she was already moving. She grabbed the hand that had the blade and shoved it against his leg. The blade went in all the way to the hilt. Lysander cried out in pain and lashed out. Pushing her back. She was shoved against the wall of the castle and then she felt herself tumble backwards even more. She caught the wall as she tumbled over and grabbed on with one hand onto one of the arrow slits just below the parapets.

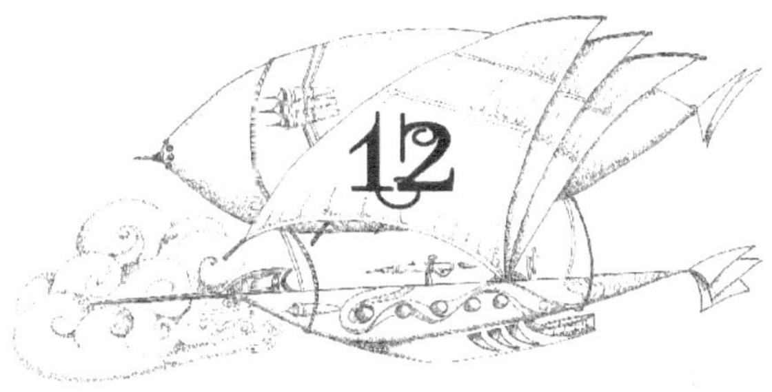

The Blazing Blunderbuss was moving away from the tower as it was struggling to keep the soldiers pinned. With only Murphy on the guns, Hara was surprised they had held their own for so long. Hara tapped Gideon's shoulder. "You need to put me down on the wall."

He hesitated but the army below was mostly charred or melted. He swooped down and held onto the wall with one hand as he shoved the soldiers aside with the other. Hara unstrapped herself and climbed over Gideon's shoulder onto the wall.

Hara said, "Go see if you can deal with Lysander. I'm going to deal with soldiers in the tower so the Blazing Blunderbuss can come in to pick us up."

Gideon's answer was to drop back off the wall and fly away from her. Hara pulled her guns out that she hadn't even used yet and went towards the tower. No one had expected her to abandon her perch on Gideon's shoulders so they were surprised as she rushed into the tower.

With the Blazing Blunderbuss on one side and her on the other, the soldiers had no chance. Especially as she heralded her entry with a couple of smoke bombs.

Hermia's fingers ached. Her heart beat heavily and all she could hear in her head was the throb of her own blood. She was going to die. There was no way they could get a rope down to her before her fingers weakened and she fell. That assumed that Lysander was in the mood to even save her life.

Lysander looked over the edge, surprised to see that she was still alive.

He said, "You stupid git, why the hell did you do that?"

Hermia was too busy trying to hold on to the stone. She wedged up her foot but it slipped. She wished she was wearing pants instead of a dress that only got in the way.

The wall shuddered around her and she wondered if the Blazing Blunderbuss had hit the wall with a cannon. All Hermia cared about was that her grip was slipping and the trembling of the wall didn't help with her grasp. Hot air washed over her and then suddenly she was gripped in a claw.

Hermia yelped as she was yanked off the wall and fell backwards. She only stopped yelling when she realised she was in the clasp of Gideon and that he was flying her away.

He flew over to the Blazing Blunderbuss and held onto the railing with one claw as he dropped her to the deck. He just let go and was off again. Hermia went to her knees, shivering with reaction. She had come so close to death. If she hadn't caught herself, she would have been splattered.

Once Hermia gathered herself, she rushed to the bridge. Henry jumped in surprise when she rushed in.

She said, "We need to get to that wall. We need to get to Lysander."

She pointed in the direction that Lysander was standing.

Murphy said, "We would love to but that part of the wall is the best defended."

"Not for long. Gideon is heading that way." Murphy swore and the whole ship tilted as Henry spun the helm.

<hr/>

Hara pleased with the results in the west tower headed towards where she had seen Lysander on the wall. She had to kick a groaning man away from the door so she could get out of the wall tower. She reloaded her guns as she went. She had several tucked in the back holsters so she had several shots before she would need to reload.

Though she mostly shot to disable rather than to kill. The soldiers weren't innocent in this but there was no need to take a life when she didn't have to.

The soldiers on the wall were focussed on Gideon, who was swooping and diving by the wall. There was no longer anyone on the ground who they had to worry about. Lysander was yelling at his men and they dared not to abandon him. There was a priest crumbled in an unconscious heap against the low wall of the parapet. There was some blood on his head but there was little Hara could do about him while the soldiers were in the way.

Hara could see in the soldier's eyes, though they knew the outcome of this battle. As Hara approached, she whistled and several soldiers looked her way. She waved with her gun. "I'm sure the duchy is going to be in a need of a new Duke really soon so you might as well collect your pay and leave."

One or two didn't hesitate and left suddenly. Some hesitated, then followed the others. Hara raised an eyebrow and one swore.

"This is not worth it."

He dropped his gun and followed the others. That was the tipping point and the rest started following. Others saw the soldiers leaving and glanced when they realised they were quickly standing alone. Some hesitated, looking at Lysander yelling at Gideon. He was red in his face and spit flying from his mouth. He was not looking like a sane, composed leader of an army. Instead, he appeared like the crazy megalomaniac he really was. Hara was worried that Lysander was about to have an apoplexy.

When most of the soldiers had left or were lowering their guns, Hara called out. "Finished pissing in the wind, Duke?"

Lysander spun around and pointed an accusing finger at her. "You! You ruined everything. I had the army. I had the girl and I was going to be an emperor. No one was in my way. Until you. I was going to get everything I deserved. I might have been born on the wrong side of the blanket but I was going to prove to everyone that I was worthy of my father's blood. That I was just as damn royal as he was."

Hara had no idea who his father was but she knew it wasn't important either. The fact that Lysander wanted to kill people to get what he deserved was the real issue.

Lysander turned to his soldiers. "Shoot her."

Hara raised her own guns and tilted her head as she took in the last of the soldiers. None of them even raised their guns. Lysander swore at them and hit one on the back of his head.

Hara whistled sharply. "It is me you have to worry about, Duke." She didn't want Lysander to hurt the soldiers merely because they had changed sides or stayed neutral. Remembering how the Duke liked to get close to people before he attacked Hara had an idea of what he was going to do.

On the airship, when they had escaped, the Duke had a gun in his hand, yet he had opted to use her as a hostage instead. Even now, the Duke didn't have any weapon of his own. His soldiers stood around him with guns. Hara had been paying attention to them before she had approached them and she knew that most of the men were actually unarmed as they needed to reload.

Hara could see the chain reaction about to happen so she stepped closer to the wall. Lysander grabbed a gun from the closest soldier. He raised it and shot. Only the soldier hadn't had time to reload. Hara had been aware of this. She had been paying attention to what was happening on the wall and apparently Lysander had not. He swore and threw the gun away.

He picked up the knife lying on the ground. It was red with blood and considering the hastily wrapped wound on his leg; she assumed it was the blade he had been injured with. Hara put her guns away and broadened her stance. This was the man she remembered from the airship. Except that he was so angry now that he wasn't thinking as a fighter, he was thinking purely through his emotions. Hara couldn't compete with him when he was fighting fit but the red cheeks and flashing eyes belied his true state of mind.

Lysander was so angry he didn't think about why she would put away her weapons and move towards the wall. She could have just shot him. Instead, she had waited for him to arm himself twice. Lysander rushed towards her with the blade. Hara sidestepped and grabbed his outstretched arm and helped the Duke over the edge of the parapet.

Lysander screamed and then the scream stopped suddenly with a wet thwack.

Gideon landed on the wall and changed into his human form. His pants were the only thing he wore. When he landed, the last of the soldiers ran.

Gideon looked over the edge. "He isn't going to be a problem anymore."

Hara shook her head. "He has already been more of a problem than we could want. We still have to find out who he told about the poison."

Gideon turned around to look at her. "That will have to wait. We need to get everyone home and I need to deal with the traitor."

Hara pressed her lips together in worry. She still didn't know who the traitor was but she had seen the toll it had taken on Gideon already, just knowing that he would have to take care of it.

Hara went over to the priest and he groaned as she knelt down next to him. He blinked his eyes in confusion. She said, "The Duke is gone. You are safe."

He asked, "The girl?" Hara looked over her shoulder to Gideon as she wasn't sure which girl the priest was talking about.

Gideon said, "I put Hermia on the ship. She was dangling from the wall when I arrived." Hara gasped at the shock of hearing how close Hermia had come to dying. She was glad she had sent Gideon when she had but she also wished she had never sent Hermia in the first place.

Hara turned back to the priest. "She is in safe hands. Do you need any help?"

The priest staggered to his feet. "Only to get out of here." Hara couldn't disagree with him. That was her plan as well.

<hr>

Liam said, "I see Talen and Alice."

He rushed off to the two as they seemed to struggle with a couple of heavy chests. The boy had too much energy. Demetrius was aching from pulled muscles from the fight they had been in at the lab.

Demetrius was about to follow Liam when Helena caught his arm and spun him around. She pressed him up against the wall and kissed him. Not just a light peck on the lips but a fiery, consuming kiss.

He was stunned for a moment, then gathered her in his arms and returned the kiss. Eventually, the kiss was over and he pulled back and blinked in confusion.

Demetrius asked, "What was that for?"

Helena smiled. "For being a hero."

Demetrius snorted. "You are the one who saved my life."

Helena still held onto him as she spoke and Demetrius had to admit that he liked the feel of her so close against him.

"And you are alright with that." Though there was a hint of a question to her voice.

So he answered, "Hell, yes. Why wouldn't I be?"

Helena stepped back and shook her head a little. "I'll explain one day, Demetrius."

Helena then followed Liam. Demetrius called after her. "So there will be another day?"

Helena glanced over her shoulder. "That is entirely up to you."

<hr>

The crew found Hara and Gideon on the wall. The Blazing Blunderbuss was moving slowly into position for them to anchor it to the wall.

Talen sighed as he dumped a chest at their feet. Hara raised an eyebrow in an unspoken question and he said, "The Duke's stash. We can't leave it here. And whoever takes over the place next probably doesn't need it."

Hara raised an eyebrow and pointed out to the valley. "But they do."

Talen said, "But…"

Hara said, "They had no say over who ruled them. They deserve every coin in that chest. They certainly worked for every coin." Even Talen could see the highly cultivated valley and the work that would have gone into clearing, planting and harvesting all those fields.

Liam dumped another chest next to the other one. Talen said, "Fine. But I want danger pay for this." Hara nodded. It was the least she could do.

Alice followed them up to the wall and Angel flew from her shoulder to Hara's.

Hara petted Angel. "Did you fight the bad men?" Angel answered with a soft, contented whirring sound.

Hara turned to Alice and asked, "Puck?"

Alice winced. "He slipped and cracked open his head. He isn't an issue but we can't question him either. We have no idea who he told about that formula you guys are worried about."

Hara shrugged. "I'm not going to be upset that he brought on his own doom." It had probably been beyond hoped that the engineer would have been reasonable and work instead for the Empire.

Hara looked at Gideon but he didn't seem worried that they couldn't question anyone on the identity of the poison producer.

Alice looked around. "Lysander?"

Hara pointed over her shoulder with her thumb and Alice looked over the wall and winced. Alice said, "Servant like master, though he really cracked open more than his head."

A rope fell from the Blazing Blunderbuss and Liam and Talen quickly worked to secure it.

Alice looked over the valley. "Are we just going to leave them like this?"

Hara said, "That isn't our problem. We will give the money to the Emperor and he can see that it goes back to the people. He owes us as we went beyond what he asked us to do. That is all we can do."

Alice nodded but it was clear she wanted to do more. The problem was that none of them could do anything. Making sure the Duke's wealth didn't get looted was actually the most helpful thing they could do.

The others climbed the ladder up into the Blazing Blunderbuss. Helena came up on the wall. She winked at the two of them and also climbed up after Alice and the boys.

Hara pointed to the two chests and said to Gideon, "You want to deal with those?"

Gideon grinned. "Oh, I love gold."

She said, "It is just temporary. It isn't part of your collection."

Gideon picked up the first chest. "I know. They are in yours." The chest disappeared out of his hands. He added as he picked up the other, "I couldn't do this kind of thing if it wasn't in your collection. It would just return to being little tiny stuff."

Hara wasn't sure what he was talking about but as long as she could give the money back later she didn't particularly care. Instead, she asked, "You honestly can't call it little tiny stuff all the time. Surely you have a name for it."

Gideon grinned. "Atoms but your people don't know about that kind of thing yet." Hara wouldn't be surprised if the dragons knew an ocean of knowledge more than humans that they kept to themselves. Hara wasn't going to argue over why dragons kept their knowledge to themselves. It was only prudent.

Demetrius finally made it on the wall and his cheeks were flushed. He hesitated by them and almost said something, then shook his head. He dashed towards the airship. It could probably wait for later, Hara realised.

Hara looked around to make sure they had everyone they needed to return to Versailles when Gideon pulled her against him. She was surprised by the sudden warmth of his flesh.

Gideon asked, "You alright with how this played out?" He was asking about her conscience. He was always concerned with her perception of a situation. She knew it wasn't because he was worried that her ethics were skewed because of her life with her father.

Instead, he knew she had a strong ethic that had been abused for years and he wanted to make sure it wasn't getting any more abused by the mayhem and adventure they had participated in.

Hara said, "I love you." Her voice filled with emotion. She wrapped her arms around his neck. "I think I'm ready. You're the best thing that has ever happened to me, Gideon."

Gideon kissed her and she melted against him. When he pulled back, he said, "You are the best thing that has happened to me as well. I would have withered away in those universities if you hadn't come to save me."

Hara stepped back. "That was the kidnappers. I just made sure you were free from them. Twice."

Gideon gave a surprised laugh. "I could have got out of both situations. Thank you very much."

Hara raised an eyebrow and placed a hand on her hip. The first time she had met Gideon, he had been trapped as a human and tied up. He had been trying to convince his captors to let him go by being annoying. She doubted he would have gotten out of that. The second time he had been waiting for her to come and rescue him. Though Hara wasn't astonished that his memory of the kidnappings differed from her own recall.

<hr>

Hara found Hermia in her room. The young woman was looking at some pants. They were obviously Liam's and Hermia was placing them against her hips to see how they'd fit.

Hara leant against the door frame and watched her for a while. When Hermia realised she wasn't alone, she looked up and smiled. "Oh, Captain, I didn't see you there."

Hara motioned to the clothing in Hermia's hands. "I doubt you will wear that at court. You would scandalise your peers. Your parents will accuse us of corrupting you. Which is probably true."

Hermia tightened her hold on the pants. She chewed on her lip and eventually said, "About that."

Hara raised an eyebrow as an invitation for Hermia to speak her mind.

"Well, I don't think I want to go home. I'd really like to pursue my studies and I want to find out who I am." Hermia rushed with the words. Hermia hesitated, then added, "I'm not cut out to be the daughter of a nobleman who is married off for political reasons. I know there is a chance I will be disowned and I know I can't ask you to help me but I know I can't go back."

Hara nodded. "Fine."

Hermia blinked in confusion. Then choked out. "Fine? No argument?"

Hara shook her head. "None. We are shorthanded as it is. You can be our new medic. Murphy said you did a really good job on his stitches. You can start your studies there." Hara motioned to the pants still in Hermia's hands. "And you can wear what you like."

Hermia let out a breath and her shoulders shook. Hara wondered if she was crying but when Hermia spoke there was emotion in her voice but no tears. "I don't know how to thank you."

Hara shook her head. "No need."

Hara turned to leave, then turned back. "Gideon is the one to thank. He was the one that suggested you'd make a good medic and that you should stay with us for a while. He has connections as a dragon so I'd suggest you butter him up a bit and see if he can get your parents to see this as a good thing."

Hermia asked, "You aren't jealous? I mean, you are suggesting I spend time with your mate."

Hara smiled. "He is my mate and nothing will change that. Don't worry about Gideon. He is mine and I am his. You can't get between that so don't even think about it."

Gideon had spent the last few months convincing Hara of that truth. As Hara spoke the words, she knew they were truth. Gideon wasn't like her father, who was always looking for the next scam and the only reason to have her around was to use her. Gideon needed her but he would never use her. Hara realised she needed Gideon as much as he needed her.

Demetrius waited until everyone was asleep before he could gather his courage and go to Helena's room. He knocked softly. If she was asleep, he didn't want to wake her. He had almost convinced himself that she was asleep and wasn't coming to the door when she eventually opened the door.

Helena was dressed in a large shirt that reached her thighs. He blushed. "I'm sorry I shouldn't have come."

Helena just looked him up and down and then caught the material at the front of his shirt and dragged him into her room.

Once inside, she lit a light and motioned for him to take a seat. He glanced at the rumpled bed but took a chair. Helena instead sat on the bed. Demetrius was determined not to look at the bed. But it was a struggle to move his eyes to a more neutral view.

Demetrius cleared his throat. "I am sorry I woke you up."

Helena said, "There are worse ways to wake up."

Demetrius blushed and he had to ask, "Do you really mean that? I mean, I need to know…" he stopped the cascade of words and took a deep breath. "I'd like to know what your feelings are about me."

Helena smiled. "You really are a gentleman. You don't try to get me in my bed, instead you ask about my feelings."

Helena tucked her feet up in the bed and pulled the blankets over herself before she settled back against the wall at the top of the bed. It was clear she was getting comfortable to talk to him for a while.

Demetrius said, "What does that mean, then?"

Helena smiled. "We will talk tonight, as I like talking to you, Demetrius, but you know there never will be anything between us. I am an ex Roshian spy and you are the son of a nobleman."

"A third son. That is nobody in noble circles." He asserted with a little more force than he had intended.

She shook her head. "We have only this time. Don't try to prolong it further. It will only hurt your family and yourself."

Demetrius felt fierce. He really liked Helena and he wanted more but he would be happy to just talk to her that night. He liked talking to her as well. Though he wasn't sure why.

He would talk to Gideon in the morning. Maybe the dragon could come up with an alternative solution than them just parting ways. Helena was the kind of person who made him feel like he was on an adventure just by being in the same room as her.

Versailles was the same but Hara felt different. She wasn't worried about dancing or dresses. Instead, she was worried about Gideon. He had been pacing and he even snapped at Angel. Even though she had admitted to Gideon that she was willing to take their relationship to the next step, she had realised that Gideon wouldn't be in the mood to do anything until he had sorted all this out. In particular, the traitor.

They were greeted in Versailles by an escort. Hara waited until the lift touched the ground before she jumped off. Harlen was with the escort. Hara eyed him suspiciously for a moment. Was he the dragon who had betrayed them all? He certainly knew about the poison and he could have found out the formula just as easily. He was close to the throne but practically nobody politically. Maybe he had wanted more power.

But Hara couldn't believe it of him. He would hurt no one in his collection. He and Gideon agreed on that in particular. That you looked after others in your collection and Harlen belonged to the largest collection along with the emperor's great grandfather. But Hara couldn't help but observe Gideon's approach of Harlen to see if Gideon would give any hint to whether he thought Harlen was the traitor. There was nothing different but maybe Gideon didn't want to telegraph that he knew who the traitor was.

Harlen said, "That was a spectacular mess."

Gideon said, "Hardly. We got rid of a seditious Duke and you can play it as fallout amongst criminals because people still think we are pirates. We got the girl back."

Harlen frowned at Hermia, who had come down as well. She was dressed in Liam's clothes and she seemed overly content about the outfit. They were a bit baggy on her but Hermia had taken a lot of them in. She would soon have a flattering wardrobe, especially if Alice did the next set of shopping. Alice had an eye for things that would flatter a person.

Harlen didn't seem nearly as impressed with the wardrobe change.

Gideon distracted Harlen before he could berate the young woman. "They had the poison, Harlen."

Harlen's look was sharp and entirely focussed on Gideon. "Are you certain?"

"I got what they had but they shared the recipe with another. I think it was a dragon hunter."

Harlen stepped closer to Gideon and Hara could see he was gritting his teeth. Hara wondered if he was angry enough to get into a fight with the messenger. Eventually, Harlen stepped down. "I will deal with it. The emperor wants to see you straight away."

Harlen motioned to the escort and several soldiers stepped forward. Hara smiled at the soldiers. "Lead the way."

Helena asked as they were walking. "Is it so important that I come along?"

Hara smiled at the young woman. "Trust me. Well, trust Gideon. He knows politics. He has a plan and it will involve you." Gideon had already told her part of what he was planning but he had kept the rest secret as he wasn't sure how much of it, he could pull off. The emperor had seemed a very reasonable man when they had met him and nothing like Gideon's brother.

Especially now that Gideon was part of the first agreement between dragons. His brother would have to take notice of Gideon and that meant that they had to set the tone of Gideon's position or Gideon's brother would use him much like a puppet like he did Harlen. Gideon would never stand for that.

They were led into an opulent study. It seemed they were still not at the level where the emperor wanted them paraded in front of the rest of the court. The emperor was signing something. He waved at his assistant to leave, then he looked up at the small group of them.

The emperor leaned back in his chair. "This wasn't the discreet mission I was expecting. I assume there is a story behind all this."

Hara said, "The Duke was working with an engineer and they had created an army of automata."

The emperor didn't seem impressed. "We have dealt with armies before."

"This army was also armed with specialised poison. Poison that only kills bonded dragons."

That had the emperor sitting forward in his chair. "Are you sure?"

Hara nodded. "We confiscated what they had. We know that others still have the recipe."

The emperor waved that off. "Grandfather will want to look into that himself. I was so sure we had the scientist under wraps. This is disturbing."

Gideon said, "If I deal with your traitor, it will make you look more powerful to my brother. He approves of people who look after his collection. But if we do this, we would expect a favour in return. Another favour, I mean."

The emperor raised an eyebrow. "And just what would that be?"

Gideon would only speak with the emperor once the others left. Hara waited outside with the others. Demetrius asked, "Is everything going to be alright?"

Hara smiled. "Probably better than alright."

The door opened and Gideon came out. Demetrius, who had been on pins and needles and was bouncing from foot to foot, asked, "What is going to happen?"

Gideon said, "Well, you, Demetrius, are going to get married."

Demetrius' face dropped. "Please don't say I still have to marry Hermia."

Gideon shook his head. "You will be marrying Helena."

Demetrius' sputtered then blushed. Helena said, "What? Why?"

Gideon said, "Well, there seems to be a new duchy opening up and the emperor needs someone there who he trusts. He can't give it to a third son as all the nobles would petition for their son to get land as well. Instead, he is giving it to the duke's common-law wife, well, widow now."

Helena stumbled a bit and Hermia held her up. She wasn't the only one stunned.

Demetrius said, "But why the marriage?"

"Well, the Emperor can't just let a Roshian spy take over a duchy. Especially one so close to the border. With her married to you, you will be the new Duke and that solves that problem."

Demetrius said to Helena, "You don't have to do this if you don't want to."

Helena blinked and Hara realised Helena was actually crying.

Gideon said, "I take it this plan pleases you, Helena."

She just nodded her head, even if it wasn't a question. Hermia asked, "What about me?"

Gideon said, "The Emperor has agreed that you need some growing up and that fostering you to another dragon family might broaden your understanding of politics, so you aren't drawn into the plans of another megalomaniac like Lysander."

Hara chuckled. "Are those your words or the emperors?"

Gideon shrugged. "Does it matter? The emperor agreed and your parents will be fools not to go along. Hermia, you can still expect them to still try to arrange a marriage for you but I'm sure we can cross that bridge when we get to it."

Hara said, "I knew you were good with politics but I like this outcome."

Gideon smiled. "And you still have your favour. Any idea what you want from the emperor?"

She shook her head. "I like having him owe me something."

Gideon just laughed at that. "He will never know what happened to him. You are more interesting than any of the dragons."

<hr>

Hermia's hands were sweating. After the Emperor's decision had come through, she had felt relief. Convincing her parents that this was a good idea was a whole other matter, though. Hermia knocked and entered the suite that her parents used when they were at court. They had come to court when she had run away and had insisted the emperor do something. They had no idea the emperor had already sent someone to collect her.

Inside, her mother was sitting on the couch. She was still dressed in her nightclothes and must have been up late the night before because it was almost lunch. Her mother squealed and jumped to her feet. She blubbered while she hugged Hermia.

Her mother was easily a watering pot but she was not very demonstrative, so Hermia wasn't sure what to do with the woman hugging her.

Eventually, Hermia got her mother sat down. Hermia's father entered the room. "What is the blather now?" He stopped when he saw her. He growled. "So, you returned. Or did the emperor's people make you return?"

Hermia stood up and her parents noticed for the first time what she was wearing.

Her mother gasped. "Oh, my dear, what are you wearing? We will have your dresses sent from home straight away."

Hermia waved it off. "No need. Because you see, the emperor has organised for me to be fostered out and these clothes are more appropriate for where I am going."

Her father wasn't pleased by that and ranted for a few minutes. Hermia winced as his volume grew.

Hermia stepped towards the door and her father said, "Where do you think you are going?"

Hermia said, "To find myself. To be someone. But don't worry, father I do appreciate the education you have given me and I won't let you down."

He blustered for a moment and Hermia used that moment to escape out of the room. Once she was outside, she gave a sigh of relief. Then with a grin on her face, she trotted to the Blazing Blunderbuss.

<hr>

emetrius asked, "You can't stay for the wedding?"

Hara shook her head. Helena was holding onto Demetrius' hand and Hara didn't doubt for a moment that the match was a good one. Even if their meeting had been filled with apathy and violence.

Hara had spoken to Helena on the ship and asked whether she really had true feelings for Demetrius, especially since she had ignored him the first time, she had met him. Helena had explained that Lysander was jealous and so she didn't look at any man, especially a man she found attractive.

Hara could understand the danger there had been with her, living with Lysander as she had. Hara just hoped they were up to the challenge of turning the Duchy around.

The two chests of gold were at Hara's feet and she motioned to them, "I'm only here to make sure these get to you. You'll need everything you can get to fix that place. You will need to lean on each other."

Helena said, "Thank you. I know it will be a long time before the people there will trust me but this will help."

Demetrius flushed. "Yes, thank you for this. I've had training but this will be the first time I've had to deal with my own people and my own accounts."

Hara looked at his glowing face. "You are looking forward to the challenge, aren't you?"

Demetrius grinned. "Yeah. I've realised that the only reason I agreed to marry Hermia was that she is an heiress and as a third son, that meant more to me than anything. Now this prize is even better."

He turned his look on Helena and Hara snorted with laughter as she realised, he meant Helena. It was clear that Helena was also aware that he meant her as she returned the smile he gave her.

Hara said, "Well, I'll leave you two lovebirds. We are heading out straight away."

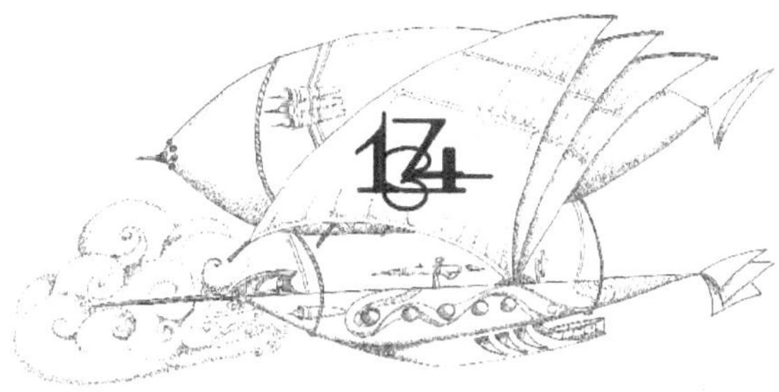

17

Gideon found Janus in the garden. He had his shoes off and his feet in the water of the pond with goldfish swimming past his feet. He didn't look up when Gideon stepped up behind him.

Gideon said, "I thought you would see us when we arrived. It was clear everyone knew we were on our way."

Janus said, "I heard."

There was a long silence and Gideon asked, "Why?"

"Your collections. You think that means everything but for someone like me, I am no one because I don't have a collection."

"You could have made your own collection. Others have." Gideon wasn't about to let him use the excuse of not having a collection for the reason he would attempt genocide.

Janus snorted. "I can't even look after myself. Why would I want to collect other things that I have to look after?"

Gideon said, "Just a little more than spiteful to kill all of us because you don't want to have a collection."

Janus looked up at Gideon. "I know but I was getting desperate. When I heard you had taken a mate, I realised I was finally at the bottom of the pecking order and I really couldn't stand it. So, I thought I would even the odds a bit."

Gideon shook his head. "They gave the recipe to a dragon hunter. You have put us all at risk." Gideon had been in a discussion with Harlen and he had asked around and had confirmed that it was the dragon hunter that Lysander had found who had the recipe. Harlen would leave this evening to chase after the dragon hunter and make sure they did not share the recipe with anyone else. Hopefully Harlen wouldn't have to slay too many humans to make sure they were safe.

Janus went back to watching the fish. "Not to me. The poison doesn't kill unbonded dragons and I have no collection let alone a mate."

Janus deserved death for what he had attempted but dragons were an endangered species and it would not be a light thing to have one of them killed. Gideon said, "I wanted to kill you but my mate reminded me that we are endangered species and no matter what, I can't have you killed."

Gideon dropped a set of cuffs on the ground. "You know they have found a new continent. You can go there and stay there alone for a while. Think about what you have done. But so you don't leave or cause any more trouble, you will wear these. Maybe when you realise how it is to really be on the bottom of the pecking order, you will appreciate all that you have."

Janus looked at the cuffs. "If I refuse?"

Gideon said, "You would have left or fought if you were thinking of taking a different path. You knew I would know it was you and you waited here."

Janus took his feet out of the water. "I suppose you are right, Gideon. I will not run or fight." He got to his feet, picking up the cuffs as he did. He put one on his wrist. "You know you were always my best friend."

Gideon said, "I know."

Janus put on the other cuff. "But I wasn't yours. You were happy to be a loner. Why didn't you stay on our home planet? You could have been perfectly alone there."

Gideon said, "I don't like to be alone. I just like to surround myself with interesting people or no one at all."

Janus looked up from his cuffs fresh on his wrists. "I'm not interesting? You slay me, Gideon. When did this happen?"

"A hundred years ago, when all you could do was drink and womanise."

Janus shrugged. "It certainly kept me entertained but I can see why you wouldn't find that interesting. I should have stuck to the science."

Gideon could only agree. Maybe then he wouldn't be exiled and a traitor.

❦

Hara cleared a drawer. "Henry said he found a job in the capital. Sad to see him go but I understand." When Gideon didn't say anything she looked over to him. He looked thoughtful. "How did it go?"

Gideon put his clothes on the bed. They were moving his things into her room. Hara hadn't wanted to ask him how things had gone with Janus until they were alone.

"As you would expect," Gideon said with a shrug of his shoulders.

Hara shook her head. "I wouldn't have thought Janus was capable of something like this. He would have only hurt his own people."

Gideon said, "I'll be honest, Hara. I don't really want to talk about Janus right now."

Hara looked up to see that Gideon's eyes were actually golden with heat. Hara held some of her underwear that she had been about to move from the drawer still in her hands. She put it down with a blush.

Gideon stepped up close to her. "I didn't think you would come to this point so quickly."

Hara wrinkled her nose. "Did I seem that stubborn?"

He shook his head and placed his hands on her waist. "Not stubborn. Protective. You have been hurt before. I'm glad you let me in."

She rested her head on his shoulder. "I'm glad I let you in as well."

"I suppose this is a good time to tell you we are taking Janus to the new continent found in the south."

Hara snorted a laugh but she didn't move his arms. She liked the way he felt against her. She could stay there forever. Considering that she was now immortal, she very well could stay like that forever.

Thank You